HUCKLEBERRY FINN

Mark Twain

Abbey Classics

© **Brown Watson** (Leicester) Ltd

PRINTED IN ROMANIA

CHAPTER ONE

Miss Watson

You don't know about me, without you have read a book by the name of "The Adventures of Tom Sawyer", but that ain't no matter. That book was made by Mr. Mark Twain, and he told the truth, mainly. There was things which he stretched, but mainly he told the truth.

Now the way that the book winds up, is this: Tom and me found the money that the robbers hid in the cave, and it made us rich. We got six thousand dollars apiece — all gold. It was an awful sight of money when it was piled up. Well, Judge Thatcher, he took it and put it out at interest, and it fetched us a dollar a day apiece, all the year round — more than a body could tell what to do with. The Widow Douglas, she took me for her son, and allowed she would civilise me; but it was rough living in the house all the time, considering how dismal regular and decent the widow was in all her ways. The widow rung a bell for supper, and you had to come to time. When you got to the table you couldn't go right to eating, but you had to wait for the widow to tuck down her head and grumble a little over the victuals, though there warn't really anything the matter with them.

After supper she got out her book and learned me about Moses and the "Bulrushers"; and I was in a sweat to find out all about him; but by-and-by she let it out that Moses

3

had been dead a considerable long time; so then I didn't care no more about him; because I don't take stock in dead people.

Pretty soon I wanted to smoke, and asked the window to let me. But she wouldn't. She said it was a mean practice and wasn't clean, and I must try to not do it any more. That is just the way with some people. They get down on a thing when they don't know nothing about it.

Her sister, Miss Watson, a tolerable slim old maid, with goggles on, had just come to live with her, and took a set at me now, with a spelling-book. She worked me middling hard for about an hour, and then the widow made her ease up. I couldn't stood it much longer.

By-and-by they had prayers, and then everybody was off to bed. I went up to my room with a piece of candle and put it on the table. Then I set down in a chair by the window and tried to think of something cheerful, but it warn't no use. I felt so lonesome I most wished I was dead.

Well, after a long time I heard the clock away off in the town go boom — boom — boom — twelve licks — and all still again — stiller than ever. Pretty soon I heard a twig snap, down in the dark amongst the trees — something was a stirring. I set still and listened. Directly I could just barely hear a "me-yow! me-yow!" down there. That was good! Says I, "me-yow! me-yow!" as soft as I could, and then I put out the light and scrambled out of the window onto the shed. Then I slipped down to the ground and crawled in amongst the trees, and sure enough there was Tom Sawyer waiting for me.

We went tip-toeing along a path amongst the trees back towards the end of the widow's garden, stooping down so as the branches wouldn't scrape our heads. When we was passing by the kitchen I fell over a root and made a noise. We scrouched down and laid still.

Then Tom said he hadn't got candles enough, and he would slip in the kitchen and get some more. I didn't want him to try. But Tom wanted to resk it; so we slid in there and got three candles, and Tom laid five cents on the table for pay.

As soon as Tom was back, we cut along the path, around the garden fence, and by-and-by fetched up on the steep top of the hill the other side of the house.

Well, when Tom and me got to the edge of the hill-top, we looked away down into the village and could see three or four lights twinkling, where there was sich folks, maybe; and the stars over us was sparkling ever so fine; and down by the village was the river, a whole mile broad, and awful still and grand. We went down the hill and found Joe Harper, and Ben Rogers, and two or three more of the boys, hid in the old tanyard. So we unhitched a skiff and pulled down the river two mile and a half, to the big scar on the hillside, and went ashore.

We went to a clump of bushes, and Tom made everybody swear to keep the secret, and then showed them a hole in the hill, right in the thickest part of the bushes. Then we lit the candles and crawled in on our hands and knees. We went about two hundred yards, and then the cave opened up. Tom poked about amongst the passages and pretty soon ducked under a wall where you wouldn't a noticed that there was a hole. We went along a narrow place and got into a kind of room, all damp and sweaty and cold, and there we stopped. Tom says:

"Now we'll start this band of robbers and call it Tom Sawyer' Gang. Everybody that wants to join has got to take an oath, and write his name in blood."

Everybody was willing. So Tom got out a sheet of paper that he had wrote the oath on, and read it. It swore every boy to stick to the band, and never tell any of its secrets;

and if anybody done anything to any boy in the band, whichever boy was ordered to kill that person and his family must do it, and he mustn't eat and he mustn't sleep till he had killed them and hacked a cross in their breasts, which was the sign of the band. And nobody that didn't belong to the band could use that mark, and if he did he must be sued; and if he done it again he must be killed. And if anybody that belonged to the band told the secrets, he must have his throat cut, and then have his carcass burnt up and the ashes scattered all around, and his name blotted off of the list with blood and never mentioned again by the gang, but have a curse put on it and be forgot, for ever.

Everybody said it was a real beautiful oath, and asked Tom if he got it out of his own head. He said, some of it, but the rest was out of pirate books, and robber books, and every gang that was high-toned had it.

Then they all stuck a pin in their fingers to get blood to sign with, and I made my mark on the paper.

"Now," says Ben Rogers, "what's the line of business of this Gang?"

"Nothing only robbery and murder," Tom said.

"Must we always kill the people?"

"Oh certainly. It's best. Some authorities think different, but mostly it's considered best to kill them. Except some that you bring to the cave here and keep them till they're ransomed."

"Ransomed? What's that?"

"I don't know. But that's what they do. I've seen it in books; and so of course that's what we've got to do."

Ben Rogers said he couldn't get out much, only Sundays, and so he wanted to begin next Sunday; but all the boys said it would be wicked to do it on Sunday, and that settled the thing. They agreed to get together and fix a day as soon as they could, and then we elected Tom Sawyer first captain and Joe Harper second captain of the Gang, and so started home.

I clumb up the shed and crept into my window just before day was breaking. My new clothes was all greased up and clayey, and I was dog-tired.

CHAPTER TWO

Playing Robbers

Well, I got a good going-over in the morning, from old Miss Watson, on account of my clothes; but the widow she didn't scold, but only cleaned off the grease and clay and looked so sorry that I thought I would behave a while if I could. Then Miss Watson she took me to the closet and prayed, but nothing come of it. She told me to pray every day, and whatever I asked for I would get it. But it warn't so. I tried it. Once I got a fish-line, but no hooks. It warn't any good to me without hooks. I tried for the hooks three or four times, but somehow I couldn't make it work. By-and-by, one day, I asked Miss Watson to try for me, but she said I was a fool. She never told me why, and I couldn't make it out no way.

Pap he hadn't been seen for more than a year and that was comfortable for me; I didn't want to see him no more. He used to always whale me when he was sober and could get his hands on me; though I used to take to the woods most of the time when he was around. Well, about this time he was found in the river drowned, about twelve miles above town, so people said. They judged it was him, anyway; said this drowned man was about his size, and was ragged, and had uncommon long hair — which was all like pap — but they couldn't make nothing out of the face, because it had been in the water so long it warn't much like a face at all. They said he was floating on his back in the water. They took him and buried him on the bank. But I warn't comfortable long, because I happened to think of something. I knowed mighty well that a drowned man don't float on his back, but on his face. So I knowed, then, that this warn't pap, but a woman dressed up in a man's clothes. So I was uncomfortable again. I judged the old man would turn up again by-and-by, though I wished he wouldn't.

We played robbers now and then about a month, and then I resigned. All the boys did. We hadn't robbed nobody; we hadn't killed any people, but only just pretended. We used to hop out of the woods and go charging down on hog-drovers and women in carts taking garden stuff to market, but we never hived any of them. Tom Sawyer called the hogs "ingots," and he called the turnips and stuff "julery," and we would go to the cave and pow-wow over what we had done and how many people we had killed and marked. But I couldn't see no profit in it.

Well, three or four months run along, and it was well into the winter, now. I had been to school most of the time, and could spell, and read, and write just a little, and could say the multiplication table up to six times seven is thirty-five, and I don't reckon I could ever get any further than that if I was to live for ever. I don't take no stock in mathematics, anyway.

At first I hated the school but by-and-by I got so I could stand it. Whenever I got uncommon tired I played hookey, and the hiding I got next day done me good and cheered me up. So the longer I went to school the easier it got to be.

I was getting sort of used to the widow's ways, too, and they warn't so raspy on me. Living in a house, and sleeping in a bed, pulled on me pretty tight, mostly, but before the cold weather, I used to slide out and sleep in the woods, sometimes, and so that was a rest to me. I liked the old ways best, but I was getting so I liked the new ones, too, a little bit. The widow said I was coming along slow but sure, and doing very satisfactory. She said she warn't ashamed of me.

One morning I happened to turn over the salt-cellar at breakfast. I reached for some of it as quick as I could, to throw over my left shoulder and keep off the bad luck, but Miss Watson was in ahead of me, and crossed me off.

There is ways to keep off some kinds of bad luck, but this wasn't one of them kind; so I never tried to do anything, but just poked along low-spirited and on the watch-out.

I went down the front garden and clumb over the stile, where you go through the high board fence. There was an inch of new snow on the ground, and I seen somebody's tracks. They had come up from the quarry and stood around the style a while, and then went on around the garden fence. It was funny they hadn't come in, after standing around so. I couldn't make it out. It was very curious, somehow. I was going to follow around, but I stooped down to look at the tracks first. I didn't notice anything at first, but next I did. There was a cross in the left boot-heel made with big nails, to keep off the devil.

I was up in a second and shining down the hill. I looked over my shoulder every now and then, but I didn't see nobody. I was at Judge Thatcher's as quick as I could get there. He said:

"Why, my boy, you are all out of breath. Did you come for your interest?"

"No, sir," I says, "is there some for me?"

"Oh, yes, a half-yearly is in, last night. Over a hundred and fifty dollar. Quite a fortune for you. You better let me invest it along with your six thousand, because if you take it, you'll spend it."

"No, sir," I says, "I don't want to spend it. I don't want it at all — nor the six thousand, nuther. I want you to take it; I want to give it to you — the six thousand and all."

He studied a while, and then he says:

"Oho-o. I think I see. You want to *sell* all your property to me — not give it. That's the correct idea."

Then he wrote something on a paper and read it over, and says:

"There — you see it says 'for a consideration.' That means I have bought it of you and paid you for it. Here's a dollar for you. Now, you sign it."

When I lit my candle and went up to my room that night, there set pap, his own self!

I had shut the door to. Then I turned around, and there he was. I used to be scared of him all the time, he tanned me so much. I reckoned I was scared now, too; but in a minute I see I was mistaken. That it, after the first jolt, as you may say, when my breath sort of hitched — he being so unexpected; but right away after, I see I warn't scared of him worth bothering about.

He was most fifty, and he looked it. His hair was long and tangled and greasy, and hung down, and you could see his eyes shining through like he was behind vines. It was all black, no grey; so was his long, mixed-up whiskers. There warn't no colour in his face, where his face showed; it was white; not like another man's white, but a white to make a body sick, a white to make a body's flesh crawl — a tree-toad white, a fish-belly white. As for his clothes — just rags, that was all. He had one ankle resting on 'tother knee; the boot on that foot was busted, and two of his toes stuck through, and he worked them now and then. His hat was laying on the floor; an old black slouch with the top caved in, like a lid.

I stood a-looking at him; he set there a-looking at me, with his chair tilted back a little. I set the candle down. I noticed the window was up; so he had clumb in by the shed. He kept a-looking me over. By-and-by he says:

"Ain't you a sweet-scented dandy, though? A bed; and bedclothes; and a look'n glass; and a piece of carpet on the floor — and your own father got to sleep with the hogs in the tanyard. I never see such a son. I bet I'all take some o'these frills out o'you before I'm done with you. Why there ain't no end to your airs — they say you're rich. Hey? — how's that?"

"Looky here — mind how you talk to me; I'm a-standing about all I can stand, now — so don't gimme no sass. I've been in town two days, and I hain't heard nothing but about you bein'rich. I heard about it away down the river, too. That's why I come. You git me that money to-morrow — I want it."

"I hain't got no money, I tell you. You ask Judge Thatcher; he'll tell you the same."

"All right. I'll ask him; and I'll make him pungle, too, or I'll know the reason why. Say — how much you got in your pocket? I want it."

"I hain't got only a dollar, and I want that to . . ."

"It don't make no difference what you want it for — you just shell it out."

Next day he was drunk, and he went to Judge Thatcher's and bullyragged him and tried to make him give up the money, but he couldn't, and then he swore he'd make the law force him.

The judge and the widow went to law to get the court to take me away from him and let one of them be my guardian; but it was a new judge that had just come, and he didn't know the old man; so he said courts mustn't interfere and separate families if they can help it; said he'd druther not take a child away from its father. So Judge Thatcher and the widow had to quit on the business.

That pleased the old man till he couldn't rest. He said he'd cowhide me till I was black and blue if I didn't raise some money for him. I borrowed three dollars from Judge Thatcher, and pap took it and got drunk and went a-blowing around and cussing and whooping and carrying on; and he kept it up all over the town, with a tin pan, till most midnight; then they jailed him, and next day they had him before court, and jailed him again for a week. But he said *he* was satisfied; said *he* was the boss of his son, and he'd make it warm ofr *him*.

CHAPTER THREE

Living with Pap

Well, pretty soon the old man was up and around again, and then he went for Judge Thatcher in the courts to make him give up that money, and he went for me, too, for not stopping school. He catched me a couple of times and thrashed me, but I went to school just the same, and dodged him or out-run him most of the time. I didn't want to go to school much, before, but I reckoned I'd go now to spite pap. That law trial was a slow business; appeared like they warn't ever going to get started on it; so every now and then I'd borrow two or three dollars off of the judge for him, to keep from getting a cowhiding. Every time he got money, he got drunk: and every time he got drunk he raised Cain around town; and every time he raised Cain he got jailed.

He was just suited — this kind of thing was right in his line.

He watched out for me one day in the spring, and catched me, and took me up the river about three mile, in a skiff, and crossed over to the Illinois shore where it was woody and there warn't no houses but on old log hut in a place where the timber was so thick you couldn't find it if you didn't know where it was.

He kept me with him all the time, and I never got a chance to run off. We lived in that old cabin, and he always locked the door and put the key under his head, nights. He had a gun which he had stole, I reckon, and we fished and hunted, and that was what we lived on. Every little while he locked me in and went down to the store, three miles, to the ferry, and traded fish and game for whisky and fetched it home and got drunk and had a good time, and licked me.

But by-and-by pap got too handy with his hick'ry, and I couldn't stand it. I was all over welts. He got to going awa yso much, too, and locking me in. Once he locked me in and was gone three days. It was dreadful lonesome. I judged he had got drowned and I wasn't ever going to get out any more. I was scared. I made up my mind I would fix up some way to leave there. I had tried to get out of that cabin many a time, but I couldn't find no way. There warn't a window to it big enough for a dog to get through. I couldn't get up the chimbly, it was too narrow. The door was thick solid oak slabs. Pap was pretty careful not to leave a knife or anything in the cabin when he was away; I reckon I had hunted the place over as much as a hundred times; well, I was 'most all the time at it, because it was about the only way to put in the time. But this time I found something at last; I found an old rusty wood-saw without any handle; it was laid in between a rafter and the clap-boards of the roof. I greased it up and went to work. There was an old horse-blanket nailed against the logs at the far end of the cabin behind the table, to keep the wind from blowing through the chinks and putting the candle out. I got under the table and raised the blanket and went to work to saw a section of the big bottom log out, big enough to let me through. Well, it was a good long job, but I was getting towards the end of it when I heard pap's gun in the woods. I got rid of the signs of my work, and dropped the blanket and hid my saw, and pretty soon pap came in.

Pap warn't in a good humour — so he was his natural self. He said he was down to town, and everything was going wrong. His lawyer said he reckoned he would win his lawsuit and get the money, if they ever got started on the trial; but then there was ways to put it off a long time, and Judge Thatcher knowed how to do it. And he said people allowed there'd be another trial to get me away from him and give me to the widow for my guardian, and they guessed it would win, this time. This shook me up considerable, because I didn't want to go back to the widow's any more and be so cramped up, and civilised, as they called it.

The old man made me go to the skiff and fetch the things he had got. There was a fifty-pound sack of corn meal, and a side of bacon, ammunition, and a four-gallon jug of whisky, and an old book and two newspapers for wadding, besides some tow.

I got the things all up to the cabin, and then it was about dark. While I was cooking supper the old man took a swig or two and got sort of warmed up and went to ripping again. He had been drunk over in town, and laid in the gutter all night, and he was a sight to look at. A body would a thought he was Adam, he was just all mud.

After supper pap took the jug, and said he had enough whisky there for two drunks and one delirium tremens. That was always his word. I judged he would be blind drunk in about an hour, and then I would steal the key, or saw myself out, one or 'tother. He drank and drank, and tumbled down on his blankets, by-and-by; but luck didn't run my way. He didn't go sound asleep but was uneasy. He groaned, and moaned, and thrashed around this way and that, for a long time. At last I got so sleepy I couldn't keep my eyes open, all I could do, and so before I knowed what I was about I was sound asleep.

"Git up!" what you'bout!"

I opened my eyes and looked around, trying to make out where I was. It was after sun-up, and I had been sound asleep. Pap was standing over me, looking sour — and sick, too.

"Out with you and see if there's a fish on the lines for breakfast. I'll be along in a minute."

He unlocked the door and I cleared out, up the river bank. I noticed some pieces of limbs and such things floating down, and a sprinkling of bark; so I knowed the river had begun to rise.

I went along up the bank with one eye out for pap and 'tother one out for what the rise might fetch along. Well, all at once, here comes a canoe; just a beauty, too, about thirteen or fourteen foot long, riding like a duck. I shot head first off the bank, like a frog, clothes and all on, and struck out for the canoe. It was a drift canoe, sure enough, and I clumb in and paddled her ashore. Thinks I, the old man will be glad when he sees this — she's worth ten dollars. But I got to shore pap wasn't in sight yet, and as I was running her into a little creek like a gully, all hung over with vines and willows, I struck another idea; I judged I'd hide her good, and then, stead of taking to the woods when I run off, I'd go down the river about fifty miles and camp in one place for good, and not have such a rough time tramping on foot.

It was pretty close to the shanty, and I thought I heard the old man coming, all the time; but I got her hid; and then I out and looked around a bunch of willows, and there was the old man down the path apiece just drawing a bead on a bird with his gun. So he hadn't seen anything.

When he got along, I was hard at it taking up a "trot" line. He abused me for being so slow, but I told him I fell in the river and that was what made me so long. I knowed he would see I was wet, and then he would be asking questions. We got five cat-fish off the lines and went home.

We laid off, after breakfast, to sleep up, both of us being wore out.

About twelve o'clock we turned out and went along up the bank. The river was coming up pretty fast, and lots of drift-wood going by on the rise. By-and-by, along comes part of a log raft — nine logs fast together. We went out with the skiff and towed it ashore. Then we had dinner. Anybody but pap would a waited and seen the day through, so as to catch more stuff; but that warn't pap's style. Nine logs was enough for one time; he must shove right over to town and sell. So he locked me in and took the skiff and started off towing the raft about half past three. I judged he wouldn't come back that night. I waited till I reckoned he had got a good start, then I out with my saw and went to work on that log again. Before he was 'tother side of the river, I was out of the hole; him and his raft was just a speck on the water away off yonder.

I took the sack of corn meal and took it to where the canoe was hid, and shoved the vines and branches apart and put it in; then I done the same with the side of bacon; then the whisky jug; I took all the coffee and sugar there was, and all the ammunition. I cleaned out the place. I wanted an axe, but there wasn't any, only the one out at the wood pile, and I knowed why I was going to leave that.

I had wore the ground a good deal, crawling out of the hole and dragging out so many things. So I fixed that as good as I could from the outside by scattering dust on the place, which covered up the smoothness and the sawdust. Then I fixed the piece of log back into its place, and put too rocks under it and one against it to hold it there.

It was all grass clear to the canoe; so I hadn't left a track. I followed around to see. I stood on the bank and looked out over the river. All safe. So I took the gun and went up a piece into the woods and was hunting around for some birds, when I see a wild pig. I shot this fellow and took him into camp.

I took the axe and smashed in the door. I beat it and hacked it considerable, a-doing it. I fetched the pig in and took him back nearly to the table and hacked into his throat with the axe, and laid him down on the ground to bleed — I say ground, because it *was* ground — hard packed, and no boards. Well, next I took an old sack and put a lot of big rocks in it — all I could drag — and I started it from the pig and dragged it to the door and through the woods down to the river and dumped it in, and down it sunk, out of sight.

Well, last I pulled out some of my hair, and bloodied the axe good, and stuck it on the back side, and slung the axe in the corner. Then I took up the pig and held him to my breast with my jacket (so he couldn't drip) till I got a good piece below the house and then dumped him into the river.

It was about dark, now; so I dropped the canoe down the river under some willows that hung over the bank, and waited for the moon to rise. I made fast to a willow; then I took a bite to eat, and by-and-by laid down in the canoe to smoke a pipe and lay out a plan. I says to myself, they'll follow the track of that sackful of rocks to the shore and then drag the

17

river for me. They'll soon get tired of that, and won't bother no more about me. All right: I can stop anywhere I want to. Jackson's Island is good enough for me; I know that island pretty well, and nobody ever comes there. And then I can paddle over to town, nights, and slink around and pick up things I want. Jackson's Island's the place.

I was pretty tired, and the first thing I knowed, I was asleep. When I woke up, I didn't know where I was, for a minute. I set up and looked around, a little scared. Then I remembered. The river looked miles and miles across. The moon was so bright I could a counted the drift logs that went a slipping along, black and still, hundred of yards out from shore. Everything was dead quiet, and it looked late, and *smelt* late. You know what I mean — I don't know words to put it in.

I took a good gap and a stretch, and was just going to unhitch and start, when I heard a sound away over the water. I listened. Pretty soon I made it out. It was that dull kind of a regular sound that comes from oars working in rowlocks when it's a still night.

Thinks I, maybe it's pap, though I warn't expecting him. He dropped below me, with the current, and by-and-by he came a-swinging up shore in the easy water, and he went by so close I could a reached out the gun and touched him. Well, it *was* pap, sure enough — and sober, too, by the way he laid to his oars.

I didn't lose no time. The next minute I was a-spinning down stream soft but quick in the shade of the bank. I made two mile and a half, and then struck out a quarter of a mile or more towards the middle of the river, because pretty soon I would be passing the ferry landing and people might see me and hail me. I got out amongst the drift wood and then laid down in the bottom of the canoe and let her float. I laid there and had a good rest and a smoke out of my pipe, looking away into the sky, not a cloud in it.

18

I was away below the ferry now. I rose up and there was Jackson's Island, about two mile and a half down stream, heavy timbered and standing up out of the middle of the river, big and dark and solid, like a steamboat without any lights.

It didn't take me long to get there. I run the canoe into a deep dent in the bank that I knowed about; I had to part the willow branches to get in; and when I made fast nobody could see the canoe from the outside.

There was a little grey in the sky, now; so I stepped into the woods and laidd own for a nap before breakfast.

CHAPTER FOUR

Jim

The sun was so high when I waked, that I judged it was after eight o'clock. I laid there in the grass and the cool shade, thinking about things and feeling rested and rather comfortable and satisfied. I could see the sun out at one or two holes, but mostly it was big trees all about, and gloomy in there amongst them. There was freckled places on the ground where the light sifted down through the leaves, and the freckled places swapped about a little, showing there was a little breeze up there. A couple of squirrels set on a limb and jabbered at me very friendly.

I was powerful lazy and comfortable — didn't want to get up and cook breakfast. Well, I was dozing off again, when I thinks I hears a deep sound of *boom !* away up the river. I rouses up and rests on my elbow and listens; pretty soon I hears it again. I hopped up and went and looked out at a hole in the leaves, and I see a bunch of smoke laying on the water a long ways up — about abreast the ferry. And there was the ferry-boat full of people, floating along down. I knowed what was the matter, now. *Boom !* I see the white smoke squirt out of the ferry-boat's side. You see, they was firing cannon over the water, trying to make my carcass come to the top.

By-and-by she come along, and she drifted in so close that they could a run out a plank and walked ashore. Most everybody was on the boat. Pap, and Judge Thatcher, and Becky Thatcher, and Joe Harper, and Tom Sawyer, and his old Aunt Polly, and Sid and Mary, and plenty more. Everybody was talking about the murder.

The boat floated on and went out of sight around the shoulder of the island. I could hear the booming, now and then, further and further, off, and by-and-by, after an hour, I didn't hear it no more. The island was three mile long. I judged they had got to the foot, and was giving it up.

I knowed I was all right now. Nobody else would come a-hunting after me. I got my traps out of the canoe and made me a nice camp in the thick woods. I made a kind of a tent out of my blankets to put my things under so the rain couldn't get at them. I catched a cat-fish and haggled him open with my saw, and towards sundown I started my camp-fire and had supper. Then I set out a line to catch some fish for breakfast.

When it was dark, I set by my camp-fire smoking, and feeling pretty satisfied; but by-and-by it got sort of lonesome, and so I went and set on the bank and listened to the currents washing along, and counted the stars and drift-logs and rafts that came down, and then went to bed; there ain't no better way to put in time when you are lonesome; you can't stay so, you soon get over it.

And so for three days and nights. No difference — just the same thing. But the next day I went exploring around down through the island. I was boss of it; it all belonged to me, so to say, and I wanted to know all about it, but mainly I wanted to put in the time. I found plenty strawberries, ripe and prime; and green summer-grapes, and green raspberries, and the green blackberries was just beginning to show. They would all come handy by-and-by, I judged.

Well, I went fooling along in the deep woods till I judged I warn't far from the foot of the island. I had my gun along, but I hadn't shot nothing; it was for protection; thought I would kill some game nigh home. About this time I mighty near stepped on a good sized snake, and it went sliding off through the grass and flowers, and I after it, trying to get a shot at it. I clipped along, and all of a sudden I bounded right on to the ashes of a camp-fire that was still smoking.

My heart jumped up amongst my lungs. I never waited for to look further, but uncocked my gun and went sneaking back on my tip-toes as fast as ever I could.

I didn't sleep much. I couldn't, somehow, for thinking. And every time I waked up I thought somebody had me by the neck. So the sleep didn't do me no good. By-and-by I says to myself, I can't live this way; I'm agoing to find out who it is that's here on the island with me; I'll find out or bust. Well, I felt better, right off.

I see the moon go off watch and the darkness begin to blanket the river. But in a little while I see a pale streak over the tree-tops, and knowed the day was coming. So I took my gun and slipped off towards where I had run across that camp-fire, stopping every minute or two to listen. But I hadn't no luck, somehow; I couldn't seem to find the place. By-and-by, sure enough, I catched a glimpse of fire, away through the trees. I went for it, cautious and slow. By-and-by, I was close enough to have a look, and there laid a man on the ground. It was getting gray daylight, now. Pretty soon he gapped, and stretched himself, and hove off the blanket, and it was Miss Watson's Jim! I bet I was glad to see him. I says:

"Hello, Jim!" and skipped out.

He bounced up and stared at me wild. Then he drops down on his kness, and puts his hands together and says:

"Doan' hurt me — don't! I hain't ever done no harm to a ghos'."

Well, I warn't long making him understand I warn't dead. I was ever so glad to see Jim. I warn't lonesome, now. I talked along, but he only set there and looked at me; never said nothing. Then I says:

"It's good daylight. Let's get breakfast. Make up your camp fire good."

So we went over to where the canoe was, and while he built a fire in a grassy open place amongst the trees, I fetched meal and bacon and coffee, and coffee-pot and frying-pan, and sugar and tin cups, and the nigger was set back considerable, because he reckoned it was all done with witchcraft. I catched a good big cat-fish, too, and Jim cleaned him with his knife, and fried him.

When breakfast was ready, we lolled on the grass and eat it smoking hot; Jim laid it in with all his might, for he was most about starved. Then when we had got pretty well stuffed, we laid off and lazied.

By-and-by Jim says:

"But looky here, Huck, who wuz it dat 'uz killed in dat shanty, ef it warn't you?"

Then I told him the whole thing, and he said it was smart. He said Tom Sawyer couldn't get up no better plan than what I had. Then I says:

"How do you come to be here, Jim, and how'd you get here?"

"Well, dey's reasons. But you wouldn't tell on me ef I' uz to tell you, would you, Huck?"

"Blamed if I would, Jim."

"Well, you see, it 'uz dis way. Ole Missus — dat's Miss Watson — she pecks on me all de time, en treats me pooty rough, but she alwuz said she wouldn' sell me down to Orleans. But I noticed dey wuz a nigger trader roun' de place considerable, lately, en I begin to git oneasy. Well, one night I creeps to de do', pooty late, en de do' warn't quite shet, en I hear ole missus tell the widder she gwyne to sell me down to Orleans, but she didn't want to, but she could git eight hund'd dollars for me, en it 'uz sich a big stack o' money she couldn' resis'. De widder she try to git her to say she wouldn' do it, but I never waited to hear de res'. I lit out mighty quick, I tell you."

"So we are both in hiding, I guess, Jim."

"Dat's right, Huck. We's two of a kind."

"Then we might as well make ourselves real comfortable."

I wanted to go and look at a place right about the middle of the island, that I'd found when I was exploring; so we started, and soon got to it, because the island was only three miles long and a quarter of a mile wide.

This place was a tolerable long steep hill or ridge, about forty foot high. We had a rough time getting to the top, the sides was so steep and the bushes so thick. We tramped and clumb around all over it, and by-and-by found a good big cavern in the rock, most up to the top on the side towards Illinois. The cavern was as big as two or three rooms bunched together, and Jim could stand up straight in it. It was cool in there. Jim was for putting our traps in there, right away, but I said we didn't want to be climbing up and down there all the time.

Jim said if we had the canoe hid in a good place, and had all the traps in the cavern, we could rush there if anybody was to come to the island, and they would never find us without dogs. And besides, he said it was going to rain, and did I want the things to get wet?

So we went back and got the canoe and paddled up abreast the cavern, and lugged all the traps up there. Then we hunted up a place close by to hide the canoe in, amongst the thick willows. We took some fish off the lines and set them again, and begun to get ready for dinner.

The door of the cavern was big enough to roll a hogshead in, and on one side of the door the floor stuck out a little bit and was flat and a good place to build a fire on. So we built it there and cooked dinner.

We spread the blankets inside for a carpet, and eat our dinner in there. We put all the other things handy at the back of the cavern. Pretty soon it darkened up and begun to thunder and lighten. It was one of these regular summer storms. It would get so dark that it looked all blue-black outside, and lovely; and the rain would thrash along by so thick that the trees off a little ways looked dim and spider-webby.

"Jim, this is nice" I says. "I wouldn't want to be nowhere else but here. Pass me along another hunk of fish and some hot corn-bread."

The river went on rising for ten or twelve days, till at last it was over the banks. The water was three or four foot deep on the island in the low places and on the Illinois bottom. On that side it was a good many miles wide, but on the Missouri side it was the same old distance across — a half a mile — because the Missouri shore was just a wall of high bluffs.

One night we catched a little section of a lumber raft — nice pine planks. It was twelve feet wide and about fifteen or sixteen feet long, and the top stood above water six or seven inches, a solid level floor.

Another night, when we was up at the head of the island, just before daylight, here comes a frame house down, on the west side. She was a two-storey, and tilted over, considerable. We paddled out and got aboard — clumb in at an upstairs window. But it was too dark to see yet, so we made the canoe fast and set in her to wait for daylight.

The light begun to come before we got to the foot of the island. Then we looked in at the window. We could make out a bed, and a table, and two old chairs, and lots of things around about on the floor; and there was clothes hanging against the wall. There was something laying on the floor in the far corner that looked like a man. So Jim says: "De man ain't asleep — he's dead. You hold still — I'll go en see."

He went and bent down and looked, and says:

"It's a dead man. Yes, indeedy; naked, too. He's ben shot in de back. I reck'n he's ben dead two er three days. Come in, Huck, but doan' look at his face — it's too gashly."

I didn't look at him at all. Jim throwed some old rags over him, but he needn't done it; I didn't want to see him. There was heaps of old greasy cards scattered around over the floor, and old whisky bottles, and a couple of masks made out of black cloth. There was two dirty calico dresses, and a sun-bonnet, and some women's underclothes, hanging against the wall, and some men's clothing, too. We put the lot into the canoe; it might come good. There was a boy's speckled straw hat on the floor; I took that too.

We got an old tin lantern, and a butcher knife without any handle, and a bran-new Barlow knife worth two bits in any store, and a lot of tallow candles, and a tin candlestick, and a gourd, and a tin cup, and a ratty old bed-quilt off the bed, and a reticule with needles and pins and beeswax and buttons and thread and all such truck in it, and a hatchet and some nails, and a fish-line as thick as my little finger, with some monstrous hooks on it, and a roll of buckskin, and a leather dog-collar, and a horse-shoe, and some vials of medicine that didn't have no label on them; and just as we was leaving, I found a tolerable good curry-comb, and Jim he found a ratty old fiddle-bow, and a wooden leg.

And so, take it all around, we made a good haul. When we was ready to shove off, we was a quarter of a mile below the island, and it was pretty broad day; so I made Jim lay down in the canoe and cover up with the quilt, because if he set up, people could tell he was a nigger a good ways off. I paddled over to the Illinois shore and drifted down most a half a mile doing it. I crept up the dead water under the bank, and hadn't no accidents and din't see nobody. We got home all safe.

CHAPTER FIVE

Jim and the Snake

After breakfast I wanted to talk about the dead man and guess out how he come to be killed, but Jim didn't want to. He said it would fetch bad luck; and besides, he said, he might come and ha'nt us.

"Now you think it's bad luck; but what did you say when I fetched in the snake-skin that I found on the top of the ridge day before yesterday? You said it was the worst bad luck in the world to touch a snake-skin with my hands. Well, here's your bad luck! We've raked in all this truck. I wish we could have some bad luck like this every day, Jim."

"Never you mind, honey, never you mind. Don't you git too peart. It's a-comin'. Mind I tell you, it's a-comin'."

It did come, too. It was a Tuesday that we had that talk. Well, after dinner Friday, we was laying around in the grass at the upper end of the ridge, and got out of tobacco. I went to the cavern to get some, and found a rattlesnake in there. I killed him, and curled him up on the foot of Jim's blanket, ever so natural, thinking there'd be some fun when Jim found him there. Well, by night I forgot all about the snake, and when Jim flung himself down on the blanket while I struck a light, the snake's mate was there, and bit him.

He jumped up yelling, and the first thing the light showed was the varmint curled up and ready for another spring. I laid him out in a second with a stick, and Jim grabbed pap's whisky jug and began to pour it down.

He was barefooted, and the snake bit him right on the heel. That all comes of my being such a fool as to not remember that whereever you leave a dead snake, its mate always comes there and curls around it. Jim told me to chop off the snake's head and throw it away, and then skin the body, and roast a piece of it. I done it, and he eat it, and said it would help cure him. He made me take off the rattles and tie them around his wrist, too. He said that that would help. Then I slid out quiet and throwed the snakes clear away amongst the bushes; for I warn't going to let Jim find out it was all my fault, not if I could help it.

Jim, sucked and sucked at the jug, and now and then he got out of his head and pitched around and yelled; but every time he come to himself he went to sucking at the jug again. His foot swelled up pretty big, and so did his leg; but by-and-by the drunk began to come, and so I judged he was all right; but I'd druther been bit with a snake than pap's whisky.

Jim was laid up for four days and nights. Then the swelling was all gone and he was around again. I made up my mind I wouldn't ever take aholt of a snake-skin again with my hands, now that I see what had come of it. Jim said he reckoned I would believe him next time. And he said that handling a snake-skin was such awful bad luck that maybe we hadn't got to the end of it yet.

Well, the days went along, and the river went down between its banks again; and about the first thing we done was to bait one of the big hooks with a skinned rabbit and set it and catch a cat-fish that was a big as a man, being six feet two inches long, and weighed over two hundred pounds. We couldn't handle him, of course; he would a flung us into Illinois. We just set there and watched him rip and tear around till he drowned.

Next morning I said it was getting slow and dull, and I wanted to get a stirring up, some way. I said I reckoned I would slip over the river and find out what was going on. Jim liked that notion; but he said I must go in the dark and look sharp. Then he studied it over and said, Couldn't I put on some of them old things and dress up like a girl? That was a good notion, too. So we shortened up one of the calico gowns and turned up my trouser-legs to my knees and got into it. Jim hitched it behind with the hooks, and it was a fair fit. I put on the sun-bonnet and tied it under my chin, und then for a body to look in and see my face was like looking down a joint of stove-pipe. Jim said nobody would know me, even in the daytime, hardly. I practised around all day to get the hang of the things, and by-and-by I could do pretty well in them, only Jim said I didn't walk like a girl; and he said I must quit pulling up my gown to get at my britches pocket. I took notice, and done better.

I started up the Illinois shore in the canoe just after dark'
and the drift of the current fetched me in at the bottom of
the town. I tied up and started along the bank. There was
a light burning in a little shanty that hadn't been lived in
for a long time, and I wondered who had took up quarters
there. I slipped up and peeped in at the window. There was
a woman about forty years old in there, knitting by a candle
that was on a pine table. I didn't know her face, she was a
stranger, for you couldn't start a face in that town that I
didn't know. Now this was lucky, because if this woman had
been in such a little town two days she could tell me all I
wanted to know; so I knocked at the door, and made up my
mind I wouldn't forget I was a girl.

"Come in," says the woman, and I did.

She says: "What might your name be?"

"Sarah Williams."

"Where 'bouts do you live? In the neighbourhood?"

"No'm, In Hookerville, seven mile below. I've walked
all the way, and I'm all tired out."

"Hungry, too, I reckon. I'll find you something."

"No'm I ain't hungry. I was so hungry I had to stop
two miles below here at a farm; so I ain't hungry no more.
It's what makes me so late. My mother's down sick, and out
of money and everything, and I come to tell my uncle Abner
Moore. He lives at the upper end of the town, she says. I
haint' ever been here before. Do you know him?"

"No; but I don't know everybody yet. I haven't lived
here quite two weeks. It's a considerable way to the upper
end of the town. You better stay here all night. Take off
your bonnet."

"No," I says, "I'll rest a while, I reckon, and go on. I ain't
afeared of the dark."

She said she wouldn't let me go by myself, but her
husband would be in by-and-by, maybe in a hour and a

half, and she'd send him along with me. Then she got to talking about her husband, and about her relations up the river, and her relations down the river; but by-and-by she dropped onto pap and the murder, and then I was pretty willing to let her clatter right along. She told about me and Tom Sawyer finding the six thousand dollars (only she got it ten) and all about pap and what a hard lot he was, and what a hard lot I was, and at last she got down to where I was murdered.

I says: "Who done it? We've heard considerable about these goings on, down in Hookerville, but we don't know who 'twas that killed Huck Finn."

"Well, I reckon there's a right smart chance of people here that'd like to know who killed him. Some thinks old Finn done it himself."

"No — is that so?"

"Most everybody thought it at first. He'll never know how nigh he come to getting lynched. But before night they changed around and judged it was done by a runaway nigger named Jim."

"Why, he —"

I stopped. I reckoned I better keep still. She run on, and never noticed I had put in at all.

"The nigger run off the very night Huck Finn was killed. So there's a reward out for him — three hundred dollars. And there's a reward out for old Finn too — two hundred dollars."

"Any ideas where the nigger's holed, up, ma'am?"

"Some folks thinks the nigger ain't far from here. I'm one of them — but I hain't talked it around. A few days ago I was talking with an old couple that lives next door in the log shanty, and they happened to say hardly anybody ever goes to that island over yonder that they call Jackson's Island. Don't anybody live there? says I. No, nobody, says they. I didn't say any more, but I done some thinking. I was pretty near certain I'd seen smoke over there, about the head of the island, a day or two before that, so I says to myself, like as not that nigger's hiding over there; anyway, says I, it's worth the trouble to give the place a hunt. I hain't seen any smoke sence, so I reckon maybe he's gone, if it was him; but husband's going over to see — him and another man."

"Is your husband going over there to-night?"

"Oh, yes. He went up town with the man I was telling you of, to get a boat and see if they could borrow another gun. They'll go over after midnight."

"Couldn't they see better if they was to wait till day-time?"

"Yes. And couldn't the nigger see better too? After midnight he'll likely be asleep, and they can slip around through the woods and hunt up his camp-fire all the better for the dark, if he's got one."

"I didn't think of that."

The woman kept looking at me pretty curious, and I didn't feel a bit comfortable. Pretty soon she says:

"What did you say your name was, honey?"

"M — Mary Williams."

Somehow it didn't seem to me that I said it was Mary before, so I didn't look up; seemed to me I said it was Sarah; so I felt sort of cornered, and was afeard maybe I was looking it, two. I wished the woman would say something more; the longer she set still, the uneasier I was. But now she says:

"Come, now, — what's your real name?"

"Wh-what, mum?"

"What's your real name? Is it Bill, or Tom, or Bob? — or what is it?"

I reckon I shook like a leaf, and I didn't know hardly what to do. But I says:

"Please to don't poke fun at a poor girl like me, mum. If I'm in the way, here, I'll —"

"No, you won't. Set down and stay where you are. I ain't going to hurt you, and I ain't going to tell on you, nuther. You just tell me your secret, and trust me. I'll keep it; and what's more, I'll help you. So'll my old man, if you want him to. You see, you're a runaway 'prentice — that's all. It ain't anything. There ain't no harm in it. You've been treated bad and you made up your mind to cut. Bless you, child, I wouldn't tell on you. Tell me all about it, now — that's a good boy."

So I said it wouldn't be no use to try to play it any longer, and I would just make a clean breast and tell her everything but she mustn't go back on her promise. Then I told her my father and mother was dead, and the law had bound me out to a mean old farmer in the country thirty mile back from the river, and he treated me so bad I couldn't stand it no longer; he went away to be gone a couple of days, and so I took my chance and stole some of his daughter's old clothes and cleared out, and I had been three nights coming the thirty miles.

"What's your real name, now?"

"George Peters, mum."

"Well, try to remember it, George. Don't forget and tell me it's Elexander before you go, and then get out by saying it's George Elexander when I catch you. You do a girl tolerable poor, but I spotted you for a boy. Now trot along, to your uncle, Sarah Mary Williams George Elexander Peters, and if you get into trouble you send word to Mrs. Judith Loftus, which is me, and I'll do what I can to get you out of it."

I went up the bank about fifty yards, and then doubled on my tracks and slipped back to where my canoe was, a good piece below the house. I jumped in and was off in a hurry. I went up stream far enough to make the head of the island, and then started across. I landed, and slopped through the timber and up the ridge and into the cavern. There Jim laid, sound asleep on the ground. I roused him out and says:

"Git up and hump yourself, Jim! There ain't a minute to lose. They're after us!"

Jim never asked no questions, he never said a word; but the way he worked for the next half an hour showed about how he was scared. By that time everything we had in the world was on our raft and she was ready to be shoved out from the willow cove where she was hid. We put out the campfire at the cavern the first thing, and didn't show a candle outside after that.

I took the canoe out from the shore a little piece and took a look, but if there was a boat around I couldn't see it, for stars and shadows ain't good to see by. Then we got out the raft and slipped along down in the shade, past the foot of the island dead still, never saying a word.

Must a been close onto one o'clock when we got below the island at last, and the raft did seem to go mighty slow. If a boat was to come along, we was going to take to the canoe and break for the Illinois shore; and it was well a boat didn't come, for we hadn't ever thought to put the gun into the canoe, or a fishing-line or anything to eat.

When the first streak of day begun to show, we tied up to a tow-head in a big bend on the Illinois side, and hacked off cotton-wood branches with the hatchet and covered up the raft with them so she looked like there had been a cave-in in the bank there.

We laid there all day and watched the rafts and steam-boats spin down the Missouri shore, and up-bound steam-boats fight the big river in the middle. I told Jim all about the time I had jabbering with that woman; and Jim said she was a smart one.

When it was beginning to come on dark, we poked our heads out of the cotton-wood thicket and looked up, and down, and across; nothing in sight; Jim took up some of the top planks of the raft and built a snug wigwam to get under in blazing weather and rainy, and to keep the things dry. Jim made a floor for the wigwam, and raised it a foot or more above the level of the raft, so now the blankets and all the traps was out of the reach of steamboat waves. Right in the middle of the wigwam we made a layer of dirt about five or six inches deep with a frame around it for to hold it to its place; this was to build a fire on in sloppy weather or chilly; the wigwam would keep it from being seen.

This second night we run between seven and eight hours, with a current that was making over four miles an hour. We had mighty good weather, as a general thing, and noth-ing ever happened to us at all, that night, nor the next, nor the next.

Every night we passed towns, some of them away up on black hillsides, nothing but just a shiny bed of lights, not a house could you see. The fifth night we passed St. Louis, and it was like the whole world lit up.

Every night, now, I used to slip ashore, towards ten o'clock at some little village, and buy ten or fifteen cents' worth of meal or bacon or other stuff to eat; and sometimes I lifted a chicken that warn't roosting comfortable, and took him along.

Mornings, before daylight, I slipped into corn fields, and borrowed a water-melon, or a mush-melon, or a pumpkin, or some new corn, or things of that kind.

We shot a water-fowl, now and then, that got up too early in the morning or didn't go to bed early enough in the evening. Take it all around, we lived pretty high.

The fifth night below St. Louis we had a big storm after midnight, with a power of thunder and lightning, and the rain poured down in a solid sheet. We stayed in the wigwam and let the raft take care of itself.

By-and-by says I, "Hel-lo, Jim, looky yonder!" It was a steamboat that had killed herself on a rock. We was drifting straight down for her. The lightning showed her very distinct. She was leaning over, with part of her upper deck above water.

Well, it being away in the night, and stormy, and all so mysterious-like, I felt just the way any other boy would a felt when I see that wreck laying there so mournful and lonesome in the middle of the river. I wanted to get aboard of her and slink around a little, and see what there was there. So I says:

"Let's land on her, Jim."

But Jim was dead against it, at first, but give in. He said we mustn't talk any more than we could help, and then talk mighty low. The lightning showed us the wreck again, just in time, and we fetched the stabboard derrick, and made fast there.

The deck was high out, here. We went sneaking down the slope of it to labboard, in the dark.

Pretty soon we struck the forward end of the skylight, and clumb onto it; and the next step fetched us in front of the captain's door, which was open, and by Jimminy, away down through the texas-hall we see a light! and all in the same second we seem to hear low voices in yonder!

Jim whispered and said he was feeling powerful sick, and told me to come along. I says, all right; and was going to start for the raft; but just then I heard a voice wail out and say:

"Oh, please don't, boys; I swear won't ever tell!"

Another voice said, pretty loud:

"It's a lie, Jim Turner. You've acted this way before. You always want more'n your share of the truck, and you've always got it, too, because you've swore 't if you didn't you'd tell. But this time you've said it jest one time too many. You're the meanest, treacherousest hound in this country."

By this time Jim was gone for the raft. I was just a-biling with curiosity; and I says to myself, Tom Sawyer wouldn't back out now, and so I won't either. I'm agoing to see what's going on here. So I dropped on my hands and knees, in the little passage, and crept aft in the dark, till there warn't but about one stateroom betwixt me and the cross-hall of the texas. Then, in there I see a man stretched on the floor and tied hand and foot, and two men standing over him, and one of them had a dim lantern in his hand, and the other one had a pistol. This one kept pointing the pistol at the man's head on the floor and saying:

"I'd like to! And I orter, too, a mean skunk!"

The man on the floor would shrivel up, and say: "Oh, please don't, Bill — I hain't ever goin' to tell."

And every time he said that, the man with the lantern would laugh, and say:

"Deed you ain't! You never said no truer thing 'n that, you bet you." And once he said: "Hear him beg! And yit if we hadn't got the best of him and tied him, he'd a killed us both. And what for? Jist for noth'n. Jist because we stood on our rights — that's what for. But I lay you ain't agoin' to threaten nobody any more, Jim Turner. Put up that pistol, Bill."

Bill says:

"I don't want to, Jake Packard, I'm for killin' him — and didn't he kill old Hatfield jist the same way — and don't he deserve it?"

Then I lit out, all in a cold sweat, and scrambled forward. It was dark as pitch there; but I said in a kind of coarse whisper, "Jim" and he answered up, right at my elbow, with a sort of moan, and I says:

"Quick, Jim, it ain't no time for fooling around and moaning; there's a gang of murderers in yonder, and if we don't hunt up their boat and set her drifting down the river so these fellows can't get away from the wreck, there's one of 'em going to be in a bad fix. But if we find their boat we can put all of 'em in a bad fix — for the Sheriff'll get 'em. Quick — hurry! I'll hunt the labboard side, you hunt the stabboard. You start at the raft, and."

"Oh! my lordy, lordy! Raf? Dey ain' no raf' no mo', she done broke loose en gone! — 'en here we is!"

CHAPTER SIX

Escaping from the Wreck

Well, I catched my breath and most fainted. Shut up on a wreck with such a gang as that! We'd got to find that boat, now — had to have it for ourselves.

We struck for the stern of the texas, and found it, and then scrabbled along forwards on the skylight, hanging on from shutter to shutter, for the edge of the skylight was in the water. When we got pretty close to the cross-hall door, there was a skiff, sure enough! I could just barely see her. I felt ever so thankful. In another second I would a been aboard of her; but just then the door opened. One of the men stuck his head out, only about a couple of feet from me, and I thought I was gone; but he jerked it in again, and says:

"Heave that blame lantern out o' sight, Bill!"

The door slammed to, because it was on the careened side; and in a half-second I was in the boat, and Jim come a tumbling after me. I out with my knife and cut the rope, and away we went!

When we was three or four hundred yards down-stream, we see the lantern show like a little spark at the texas door, for a second and we knowed by that the rascals had mised their boat.

Then Jim manned the oars, and we took out after our raft. Pretty soon it begun to storm again, and this time worse that ever. After a long time the rain let up, but the clouds staid, and the lightning kept whimpering, and by-and-by a flash showed us a black thing ahead, floating, and we made for it.

It was the raft, and mighty glad was we to get abord of it again. We seen a light, now, away down to the right, on shore. So I said I would go for it. The skiff was half full of plunder which that gang had stole, there on the wreck. We hustled it onto the raft in a pile, and I told Jim to float it along, and show a light when he judged he had gone about two mile, and keep it burning till I come; then I manned my oars and shoved for the light. As I got down towards it, three or four more showed — up on a hillside. It was a village. I closed in above the shore-light, and laid on my oars and floated. As I went by, I see it was a lantern hanging on the jackstaff of a double-hull ferry-boat. I skimmed around for the watchman, a-wondering whereabouts he slept; and by-and-by I found him roosting on the bitts, forward, with his head down between his knees. I give his shoulder two or three little shoves, and begun to cry.

He stirred up, in a kind of starlish way; but when he see it was only me, he took a good gap and stretch, and then he says:

"Hello, what's up? Don't cry, bub. What's the trouble?"

I says:

"Pap, and mam, and sis, and —"

Then I broke down. He says:

"Oh, dang it, now, don't take on so, we all has to have our troubles and this'n'll come out all right. What's the matter with 'em?"

"They're in an awful peck of trouble, and —"

"Where are they?"

"On the wreck."

"What, you don't mean the *Walter Scott?*"

"Yes."

"Good land! What are they doin' there, for gracious sakes?"

"Well, they didn't go there a-purpose."

"Looky here, you break for that light over yonder-way, and turn out west when you git there, and about a quarter of a mile out you'll come to the tavern. I'm agoing up around the corner here, to roust out my engineer."

I struck for the light, but as soon as he turned the corner I went back and got into my skiff and bailed her out. I was feeling rather comfortable on acounts of taking all this trouble for that gang, for not many would a done it. I wished the widow knowed about it; I judged she would be proud of me for helping these rapscallions, because rapscallions and dead beats is the kind the widow and good people takes the most interest in.

It did seem a powerful long time before Jim's light showed up; and when it did show, it looked like it was beginning to get a little gray in the east; so we struck for an island, and hid the raft, and sunk the skiff and turned in and slept like dead people.

By-and-by, when we got up, we turned over the truck the gang had stole off of the wreck, and found boots, and blankets, and clothes, and all sorts of other things, and a lot of books, and a spy-glass, and three boxes of seegars. We hadn't ever been this rich before, in neither of our lives. The seegars was prime. We laid off all the afternoon in the woods talking, and me reading the books, and having a general good time. I told Jim all about what happened inside the wreck, and at the ferry-boat; and I said these kinds of things was adventures; but he said he didn't want no more adventures.

We judged that three nights more would fetch us to Cairo, at the bottom of Illinois, where the Ohio River comes in, and that was what we was after. We would sell the raft and get on a steamboat and go way up the Ohio amongst the free States, and then be out of trouble.

We slept most all day, and started out at night, a little ways behind a monstrous long raft that was as long going by as a procession. She had four long sweeps at each end, so we judged she carried as many as thirty men, likely. She had five big wigwams aboard, wide apart, and an open camp-fire in the middle, and a tall flag-pole at each end. There was a power of style about her. It amounted to something being a raftsman on such a craft as that.

We went drifting down into a big bend, and the night clouded up and go hot. The river was very wide, and was walled with solid timber on both sides; you couldn't see a break in it hardly ever, or a light. We talked about Cairo, and wondered whether we would know in when we got to it.

Jim said if the two big rivers joined together there, that would show. But I said maybe we might think we was passing the foot of an island and coming into the same old river again. That disturbed Jim — and me too. So the question was, what to do? I said, paddle ashore the first time a light showed, and tell them pap was behind, coming along with a trading-scow, and was a green hand at the business, and wanted to know how far it was to Cairo. Jim thought it was a good idea, so we took a smoke on it and waited.

I went to looking out sharp for a light, and sort of singing to myself. By-and-by one showed. Jim sings out:

"We's safe, Huck, we's safe! Jump up and crack yo' heels, dat's de good ole Cairo at las', I jis knows it!"

I says:

"I'll take the canoe and go see, Jim. It mightn't be, you know."

He jumped and got the canoe ready, and put his old coat in the bottom for me to set on, and give me the paddle; and as I shoved off, he says:

"Pooty soon I'll be a-shout'n for joy, en I'll say, it's all on account o' Huck; I's a free man, en I couldn't ever ben free ef it hadn' ben for Huck."

Right then, along comes a skiff with two men in it, with guns, and they stopped and I stopped. One of them says:

"What's that, yonder?"

"A piece of a raft," I says.

"Do you belong on it?"

"Yes, sir."

"Any men on it?"

"Only one, sir."

"I reckon we'll go and see for ourselves."

"I wish you would," says I, "because it's pap that's there, and maybe you'd help me tow the raft ashore where the light is. He's sick — and so is mam and Mary Ann."

They stopped pulling. It warn't but a mighty ways to the raft, now. One says:

"Boy that's a lie. What is the matter with your pap? Answer up square, now, and it'll be the better for you."

"Well, says I, a-blubbering." "I've told everybody before, and then they just went away and left us."

"Poor devil, there's something in that. We are right down sorry for you, but we — well, hang it, we don't want the small-pox, you see. Say — I reckon your father's poor, and I'm bound to say he's in pretty hard luck. Here — I'll put a twenty dollar gold piece on this board, and you get it when it floats by. I feel mighty mean to leave you, but my kingdom! it won't do to fool with small-pox, don't you see?"

"Hold on, Parker," says the other man, "here's a twenty to put on the board for me. Good-bye, boy, and you'll be all right."

"Good bye, sir," says I.

They went off and I got aboard the raft, feeling bad and low, because I knowed very well I had done wrong.

I went into the wigwam; Jim warn't there. I looked all around; he warn't anywhere. I says:

"Jim!"

"Here I is, Huck. Is dey out o' sight yit? Don't talk loud."

He was in the river, under the stern oar, with just his nose out.

I told him they was out of sight, so he come aboard. He says:

"I was a-listening' to all de talk, en I slips into de river en was gwyne to shove for sho' if dey come aboard. But lawsy, how you did fool 'em, Huck! I tell you, chile, I 'speck it save ole Jim — ole Jim ain't gwyne to forgit you for dat, honey."

Then we talked about the money. It was a pretty good raise, twenty dollars apiece. Jim said we could take deck passage on a steamboat now, and the money would last us as far as we wanted to go in the free States. He said twenty mile more warn't far for the raft to go, but he wished we was already there.

Well, the night got grey, and ruther thick, which is the next meanest thing to fog. You can't tell the shape of the river, and you can't see no distance. It got to be very late and still, and then along comes a steamboat up the river. We lit the lantern, and judged she would see it.

We could hear her pounding along, but we didn't see her good till she was close. She aimed right for us. Often they do that and try to see how close they can come without touching; sometimes the wheel bites off a sweep, and then the pilot sticks his head out and laughs, and thinks he's mighty smart. Well, here she comes, and we said he was going to try to shave us; but she didn't seem to be sheering off a bit. There was a yell at us, and a jingling of bells to stop the engines, a pow-wow of cussing, and whistling of steam — and as Jim went overboard on one side and I on the other, she come smashing straight through the raft.

I dived — and I aimed to find the bottom, too, for a thirty-foot wheel had to go over me, and I wanted it to have plenty of room. I could always stay under water a minute; this time I reckon I staid under water a minute and a half. Then I bounced for the top in a hurry, for I was nearly busting. I popped out to my arm-pits and blowed the water out of my nose, and puffed a bit. Of course there was a booming current; and of course that boat started her engines again ten seconds after she stopped them, for they never cared much for raftsmen.

I sung out for Jim about a dozen times, but I didn't get any answer; so I grabbed a plank that touched me while I was "treading water", and struck out for shore, shoving it ahead of me. But I made out to see that the drift of the current was towards the lefthand shore, which meant that I was in a crossing; so I changed off and went that way.

It was one of these long, slanting, two-mile crossings; so I was a good long time in getting over. I made a safe landing, and clumb up the bank. I couldn't see but a little ways, but I went poking along rough ground for a quarter of a mile or more, and then I run across a big old-fashioned double log house before I noticed it. I was going to rush by and get away, but a lot of dogs jumped out and went to howling and barking at me, and I knowed better than to move another peg.

CHAPTER SEVEN

An Evening Call

About half a minute somebody spoke out of a window, without putting his head out, and says:

"Be done, boys! Who's there?"

I says:

"It's me."

"Who's me?"

"George Jackson, sir."

"What are you prowling around here this time of night for — hey?"

"I warn't prowling around, sir; I fell overboard off of the steamboat."

"Oh, you did, did you? Strike a light there, somebody."

"All ready."

"Now, George Jackson, do you know the Shepherdsons?"

"No, sir — I never heard of them."

"Well, that may be so, and it mayn't. Now, all ready. Step forward, George Jackson. And mind, don't you hurry, — come mighty slow."

I didn't hurry, I couldn't if I'd a wanted to. I took one slow step at a time, and there warn't a sound, only I thought I could hear my heart. I put my hand on the door and pushed it a little and a little more, till somebody said, "There, that's enough — put your head in." I done it, but judged they would take it off.

The candle was on the floor, and there they all was, looking at me, and me at them, for about a quarter of a minute. Three big men with guns pointed at me, which made me wince, I tell you; the oldest, grey and about sixty, the other two thirty or more — all of them fine and handsome — and the sweetest old grey-headed lady, and back of her two young women which I couldn't see right well.

The old gentleman says: "There — I reckon it's all right. Come in."

As soon as I was in, the old gentleman he locked the door and barred it and bolted it, and told the young men to come in with their guns, and they all went in a big parlour that had a new rag carpet on the floor, and got together in a corner that was out of range of the front windows — there warn't none on the side. They held the candle, and took a good look at me, and all said, "Why he ain't a Shepherdson — no, there ain't any Shepherdson about him."

The old lady says: "Why bless you, Saul, the poor thing's as wet as he can be; and don't you reckon it many be he's hungry?"

"True for you, Rachel — I forgot."

So the old lady says:

"Betsy" (this was a nigger woman), "you fly around and get him something to eat, as quick as you can, poor thing; and one of you girls go and wake up Buck and tell him — Oh, here he is himself. Buck, take this little stranger and get the wet clothes off from him and dress him up in some of yours that's dry."

When we got upstairs to his room, he got me a coarse shirt and a roundabout and pants of his, and I put them on. While I was at it he asked me what my name was, but before I could tell him, he started to telling me about a blue jay and a young rabbit he had catched in the woods day before yesterday.

"Are you all ready? All right — come along, old hoss," he says, friendly-like.

Cold corn-pone, cold corn-beef, butter, and butter-milk — that is what they had for me down there, and there ain't nothing better that ever I've come across yet.

They all asked me questions, and I told them how pap and me and all the family was living on a farm down at the bottom of Arkansaw, and my sister Mary Ann run off and got married and never was heard of no more, and Bill went to hunt them and he warn't heard of no more, and Tom and Mort died, and then there warn't nobody but just me and pap left, and he was just trimmed down to nothing, on account of his troubles; so when he died I took what there was left, because the farm didn't belong to us, and started up the river, deck passage, and fell overboard; and that was how I come to be here. So they said I could have a home there as long as I wanted it. Then it was most daylight, and everybody went to bed, and I went to bed with Buck.

It was a mighty nice family, and a mighty nice house, too. I hadn't seen no house out in the country before that was so nice and had so much style. It didn't have a iron latch on the front door, nor a wooden one with a buckskin string, but a brass knob to turn, the same as houses in a town. There warn't no bed in the parlour, not a sign of a bed; but heaps of parlours in towns has beds in them. There was a big fireplace that was bricked on the bottom, and the bricks was kept clean and red by pouring water on them and scrubbing them with another brick; sometimes they washed them over with red water-paint that they call Spanish-brown, same as they do in town. They had big brass dog-irons that could hold up a saw-log. There was a clock on the middle of the mantel-piece, with a picture of a town painted on the bottom half of the glass front, and a round place in the middle of it for the sun, and you could see the pendulum swing behind it. It was beautiful to hear that clock tick.

They had pictures hung on the walls — mainly Washingtons and Lafayettes, and battles, and Highland Marys, and one called *Signing the Declaration*. There was some that they called crayons, which one of the daughters which was dead made her own self when she was only fifteen years old.

There was beautiful curtains on the windows; white, with pictures painted on them, of castles with vines all down the walls, and cattle coming down to drink. There was a little old piano, too, that had tin pans in it, I reckon, and nothing was ever so lovely as to hear the young ladies sing *The Last Link Is Broken* and play *The Battle of Prague* on it. The walls of all the rooms was plastered, and most had carpets on the floors, and the whole house was whitewashed on the outside.

It was a double house, and the big open place betwixt them was roofed and floored, and sometimes the table was set there in the middle of the day, and it was a cool, comfortable place. Nothing couldn't be better. And warn't the cooking good, and just bushels of it, too!

Colonel Grangerford was a gentleman, you see. He was very tall and very slim, and had a darkish-paly complexion, not a sign of red in it anywheres; he was clean-shaved every morning, all over his thin face, and he had the thinnest kind of lips, and the thinnest kind of nostrils, and a high nose, and heavy eyebrows, and the blackest kind of eyes, sunk so deep back that they seemed like they was looking out of caverns at you, as you may say. His forehead was high, and his hair was black and straight, and hung to his shoulders.

There warn't no frivolishness about him, not a bit, and he warn't ever loud. He was as kind as he could be — you could feel that, you know, and so you had confidence.

Everybody loved to have him around, too; he was sunshine most always — I mean he made it seem like good weather. When he turned into a cloud-bank it was awful dark for half a minute, and that was enough; there wouldn't nothing go wrong again for a week.

When him and the old lady come down in the morning, all the family got up out of their chairs and give them goodday, and didn't get down again till they had set down.

Bob was the oldest, and Tom next. Tall, beautiful men with very broad shoulders and brown faces, and long black hair and black eyes. They dressed in white linen from head to foot, like the old gentleman, and wore broad Panama hats.

Then there was Miss Charlotte, she was twenty-five, and tall and proud and grand, but as good as she could be, when she warn't stirred up; but when she was, she had a look that would make you wilt in jour tracks, like her father. She was beautiful.

So was her sister, Miss Sophia, but it was a different kind. She was gentle and sweet, like a dove, and she was only twenty.

This was all there was of the family, now; but there used to be more — three sons; they got killed; and Emmeline that died.

There was another clan of aristocracy around there — five or six families — mostly of the name of Shepherdson. They was as hightoned, and wellborn, and rich and grand, as the tribe of Grangerfords. The Shepherdsons and the Grangerfords used the same steamboat landing, which was about two mile above our house; so sometimes when I went up there with a lot of our folks I used to see a lot of the Shepherdsons there, on their fine horses.

One day Buck and me was away out in the woods, hunting, and heard a horse coming. We was crossing the road. Buck says: "Quick! Jump for the woods!"

We done it, and then peeped down the woods through the leaves. Pretty soon a splendid young man come galloping down the road, setting his horse easy and looking like a soldier. He had his gun across his pommel. I had seen him before. It was young Harney Shepherdson. I heard Buck's gun go off at my ear, and Harney's hat tumbled off from his head. He grabbed his gun and rode straight to the place where we was hid. But we didn't wait. We started through the woods on a run. The woods warn't thick, so I looked over my shoulder, to dodge the bullet, and twice I seen Harney cover Buck with his gun; and then he rode away the way he come — to get his hat, I reckon, but I couldn't see. We never stopped running till we got home. The old gentleman's eyes blazed a minute when he heard our news — 'twas pleasure, mainly, I judged — then his face sort of smoothed down, and he says, kind of gentle:

"I don't like that shooting from behind a bush. Why didn't you step into the road, my boy?"

"The Shepherdsons don't, father. They always take advantage."

Miss Charlotte she held her head up like a queen while Buck was telling his tale, and her nostrils spread and her eyes snapped. The two young men looked dark, but never said nothing. Miss Sophia she turned pale, but the colour came back when she found the man warn't hurt.

Soon as I could get Buck down by the corn-cribs under the trees by ourselves, I says:

"Did you want to kill him, Buck?"

"Well, I bet I did."

"What did he do to you?"

"Him? He never done nothing to me."

"Well, then, what did you want to kill him for?"

"Why, nothing — only it's on account of the feud."

"Has this one been going on long, Buck?"

"Well, I should *reckon!* It started thirty year go, or som'ers along there. There was trouble 'bout something and then a lawsuit to settle it; and the suit went agin one of the men, and so he up and shot jthe man that won the suit — which he would naturally do, of course. Anybody would."

"What was the trouble about, Buck? — land?"

"I reckon maybe — I don't know."

"Well, who done the shooting? Was it a Grangerford or a Shepherdson?"

"Laws, how do I know? It was so long ago."

"Don't anybody know?"

"Oh, yes, pa knows, I reckon, and some of the other old folks; but they don't know now what the row was about in the first place."

"Has there been many killed, Buck?"

"Yes — right smart chance of funerals. But they don't always kill. Pa's got a few buck-shot in him; but he don't mind it 'cuz he don't weight much anyway. Bob's been carved up some with a bowie, and Tom's been hurt once or twice."

Next Sunday we all went to church, about three mile, everybody a-horseback. The men took their guns along, so did Buck, and kept them between their knees or stood them handy against the wall. The Shepherdsons done the same. It was pretty ornery preaching — all about brotherly love, and such-like tiresomeness; but everybody said it was a good sermon, and they all talked it over going home.

About an hour after dinner everybody was dozing around, some in their chairs and some in their rooms, and it got to be pretty dull. Buck and a dog was stretched out on the grass in the sun, sound asleep. I went up to our room, and judged I would take a nap myself. I found that sweet Miss Sophia standing in her door, which was next to ours, and she took me in her room and shut the door very soft, and asked me if I liked her, and I said I did; and she asked me if I would do something for her and not tell anybody, and I said I would. Then she said she'd forgot her Testament, and left it in the seat at church, between two other books, and would I slip out quiet and go there and fetch it to her, and not say nothing to nobody. I said I would. So I slid out and slipped off up the road, and there warn't anybody at the church, except maybe a hog or two, for there warn't any lock on the door.

Says I to myself something's up — it ain't natural for a girl to be in such a sweat about a Testament; so I give it a shake, and out drops a little piece of paper with *"Half-past two"* wrote on it with a pencil. I ransacked it, but couldn't find anything else. I couldn't make anything out of that, so I put the paper in the book again, and when I got home and upstairs, there was Miss Sophia in her door waiting for me. She pulled me in and shut the door; then she looked in the Testament till she found the paper, and as soon as she read it she looked glad; and before a body could think, she grabbed me and gave me a squeeze, and said I was the best boy in the world, and not to tell anybody.

I went off down to the river, studying over this thing. and pretty soon I noticed that my nigger was following along behind. When we was out of sight of the house, he looked back and around a second, and then comes a-running, and says:

"Mars Jawge, if you'll come down into de swamp, I'll show you a whole stack o' water-moccasins."

I followed a half a mile, then he struck out over the swamp and waded ankle-deep as much as another half-mile. We come to a little flat piece of land which was dry and very thick with trees and bushes and vines, and he says:

"You shove right in dah, jist a few steps, Mars Jawge, dah's whah dey is. I's seed em 'befo'. I don't k'yer to see 'em no mo'."

Then he slopped right along and went away, and pretty soon the trees hid him. I poked into the place a-ways, and come to a little open patch as big as a bedroom, all hung around with vines, and found a man laying there asleep — and by jings it was my old Jim!

I waked him up, and I reckoned it was going to be a grand surprise to him to see me again, but it warn't. He nearly cried, he was so glad, but he warn't surprised. Said he swum along behind me that night, and heard me yell every time, but dasn't answer, because he didn't want nobody to pick *him* up, and take him into slavery again. Says he:

"I got hurt a little, en couldn't swim fas', so I wuz a considable ways behine you, towards de las'; when you landed I reck'ned I could ketch up wid you on de lan' 'dout havin' to shout at you, but when I see dat house I begin to go slow. I 'uz off too far to hear what dey say to you — I wuz 'fraid o' de dogs — but when it 'uz all quiet agin, I knowed you's in de house, so I struck out for de woods to wait for day. Early in de mawnin' some er de niggers come along, gwyne to de fields, en dey tuck me en showed me dis place, whah de dogs can't track me on accounts o' de water, en dey brings me truck to eat every night, en tells me how you's a gitt'n along."

"Why, didn't you tell my Jack to fetch me here sooner, Jim?"

"Well, 'twarn't no use to 'sturb you, Huck, tell we could do sumfin — but we's all right, now. I ben a-buyin' pots en pans en vittles, as I got a chanst, en a-patchin' up de raf', nights, when —"

"*What* raft, Jim?"

"Our ole raf'."

"You mean to say our old raft warn't smashed all to flinders?"

"No, she warn't. She was tore up a good deal — one en' of her was — but dey warn't no great harm done, on'y our traps was mos' all los'. Ef we had'n dive so deep en swum so fur under water, en de night had'n been so dark, en we warn'n so sk'yerd, en ben sich punkin-heads, as de sayin' is, we'd a seed de raf'. But it's jis' as well we didn't, 'kase now she's all fixed up agin mos' as good as new, en we's got a new lot o' stuff, too, in de place o' what 'uz los'."

,,Why, how did you get hold of the raft again, Jim — did you catch her?"

"How I gwyne to ketch her, en I out in de woods? No, some or de niggers foun' her ketched on a snag, along heah in de ben', en dey did her in a crick, 'mongst de willows, en dey wuz so much jawin' 'bout which un 'um she b'long to de mos', dat I come to heah 'bout it pooty soon, so I ups en settles de trouble by tellin' 'um she don't b'long to none uv um', but to you en me; en I ast 'm if dey gwyne to grab a young white genlman's propaty, en git a hid'n for it?"

I don't want to talk much about the next day. I reckon I'll cut it pretty short. I waked up about dawn, and was agoing to turn over and go to sleep again, when I noticed how still it was — didn't seem to be anybody stirring. Well, I gets up, a-wondering, and goes downstairs — nobody around; everything is still as a mouse. Just the same outside; thinks I, what does it mean? Down by the wood-pile I comes across my Jack, and says:

"What's it all about?"

Says he:

"Don't you know, Mars Jawge?"

"No," I says, "I don't."

"Well, den, Miss Sophia's run off! 'deed she has. She run off in de night, sometime — nobody don't know jis' when — run off to git married to dat young Harney Shepherdson, you know — leastways, so dey 'spec. De fambly foun' it out, 'bout half an hour ago — maybe a little mo' — en' I tell you dey warn't no time los'. Sich another hurryin' up guns en hosses you never see! De women folks has gone for to stir up de relations, en ole Mars Saul en de boys tuck dey guns en rode up de river road for to try to ketch dat young man en kill him 'fo' he kin git acrost de river wid Miss Sophia. I reck'n dey's gwyne to be mighty rough times."

I took up the river road as hard as I could put. By-and-by I begin to hear guns a good ways off. When I came in sight of the log store and the wood-pile where the steamboats land, I worked along under the trees and brush till I got a good place, and then I clumb up up into the forks of a cotton-wood that was out of reach, and watched.

There was four or five men cavorting around on their horses in the open place before the log store, cussing and yelling, and trying to get at a couple of young chaps that was behind the wood-rank along-side of the steamboat landing — but they couldn't come it. Every time one of them showed himself on the river side of the wood-pile he got shot at. The boys was squatting back behind the pile, so they could watch both ways.

By-and-by the men stopped cavorting around and yelling. They started riding towards the store; then up gets one of the boys, draws a steady bead over the wood-rank, and drops one of them out of his saddle. All the men jumped off of their horses and grabbed the hurt one and started to carry him to the store; and that minute the two boys started on the run. They got half-way to the tree I was in before the men noticed. Then the men see them, and jumped on their horses and took out after them. They gained on the boys, but it didn't do no good, the boys had too good a start; they got to the wood-pile that was in front of my tree, and slipped in behind it, and so they had the bulge on the men again. One of the boys was Buck, and the other was a slim young chap about nineteen years old.

The men ripped around a while, and then rode away. As soon as they was out of sight, I sung out to Buck and told him. He didn't know what to make of my voice coming out of the tree, at first. He was awful surprised. He told me to watch out sharp and let him know when the men come in sight again.

He said his father and his two brothers was killed, and two or three of the enemy. Said the Shepherdsons laid for them, in ambush. Buck said his father and brothers ought to waited for their relations — the Shepherdsons was too strong for them. I asked him what was become of young Harney and Miss Sophia. He said they'd got across the river and was safe.

All of a sudden, *bang! bang! bang!* goes three or four guns — the men had slipped around through the woods and come in from behind without their horses! The boys jumped for the river — both of them hurt — and as they swum down the current the men run along the bank shooting at them and singing out, "Kill them, kill them!"

I was mighty down-hearted; so I made up my mind I wouldn't ever go anear that house again, because I reckoned I was to blame, somehow. I judged that that piece of paper meant that Miss Sophia was to meet Harney somewheres at half-past two and run off; and I judged I ought to told her father about that paper and the curious way she acted, and then maybe he would a locked her up and this awful mess wouldn't ever happened.

When I got down out of the tree, I crept along down the river bank a piece, and found the two bodies laying in the edge of the water, and tugged at them till I got them ashore; then I covered up their faces, and got away as quick as I could. I cried a little when I was covering up Buck's face, for he was mighty good to me.

It was just dark, now. I never went near the house, but struck through the woods and made for the swamp. Jim warn't on his island, so I tramped off in a hurry for the crick, and crowded through the willows, red-hot to jump aboard and get out of that awful country — the raft was gone! My souls, but I was scared! I couldn't get my breath for most a minute. Then I raised a yell. A voice not twenty-five foot from me, says:

"Good lan'! Is dat you, honey? Doan' make no noise."

It was Jim's voice — nothing ever sounded so good before. I run along the bank a piece and got aboard, and Jim he grabbed me and hugged me, he was so glad to see me.

I never felt easy till the raft was two [mile below there and out in the middle of the Mississippi. Then we hung up our signal lantern, and judged that we was free and safe once more. I hadn't had a bite to eat since yesterday, so Jim he got out some corn-dodgers and buttermilk, and pork and cabbage and greens — there ain't nothing in the world so good, when it's cooked right — and whilst I eat my supper we talked, and had a good time. I was powerful glad to get away from the feuds, and so was Jim to get away from the swamp. We said there warn't no home like a raft, after all.

CHAPTER EIGHT

The Duke of Bridgewater

Two or three days and nights went by; I reckon I might say they slid along so quiet and smooth and lovely.

Sometimes we'd have that whole river all to ourselves for the longest time. Yonder was the banks and the islands, across the water; and maybe a spark — which was a candle in a cabin window — and sometimes on the water you could see a spark or two — on a raft or a scow, you know; and maybe you could hear a fiddle or a song coming over from one of them crafts. It's lovely to live on a raft. We had the sky, up there, all speckled with stars, and we used to lay on our backs and look up at them, and discuss about whether they was made, or just happened — Jim he allowed they was made, but I allowed they happened; I judged it would have took too long to *make* so many. Jim said the moon could a *laid* them; well, that looked kind of reasonable, so I didn't say nothing against it, because I've seen a frog lay most as many, so of course it could be done. We used to watch the stars that fell, too, and see them streak down. Jim allowed they'd got spoiled and was hove out of the nest.

One morning about day-break, I found a canoe and crossed over a chute to the main shore — it was only two hundred yards — and paddled about a mile up a crick amongst the cypress woods, to see if I couldn't get some berries. Just as I was passing a place where a kind of cow-path crossed the crick, here comes a couple of men tearing up the path as tight as they could foot it. I was about to dig out from there in a hurry, but they was pretty close to me then, and sung out and begged me to save their lives — said they hadn't been doing nothing, and was being chased for it — said there was men and dogs a-coming.

Soon as they was aboard I lit out for our tow-head, and in about five or ten minutes we heard the dogs and the men away off, shouting. We heard them come along towards the crick, but couldn't see them; they seemed to stop and fool around a while; then, as we got further and further away all the time, we couldn't hardly hear them at all; by the time we had left a mile of woods behind us and struck the river, everything was quiet, and we paddled over to the tow-head and hid in the cotton-woods and was safe.

One of these fellows was about seventy, or upwards, and had a bald head and very grey whiskers. He had an old battered-up slouch hat on, and a greasy blue woollen shirt, and ragged old blue jeans britches stuffed into his boot tops, and home-knit galluses — no, he only had one. He had an old long-tailed blue jeans coat with slick brass buttons, flung over his arm, and both of them had big fat ratty-looking carpet-bags.

The other fellow was about thirty and dressed about as ornery. After breakfast we all laid off and talked, and the first thing that come out was that these chaps didn't know one another.

"What got you into trouble?" says the baldhead to t'other chap.

"Well, I'd been selling an article to take the tartar off the teeth — and it does take it off, too, and generaly the enamel along with it — but I stayed about one night longer than I ought to. That's the whole yarn — what's yourn?"

"Well, I'd been a-runnin' a little temperance revival thar, 'bout a week, and was the pet of the women-folks, big and little, for I was makin' it mighty warm for the rummies, I tell you, and takin' as much as five or six dollars a night — ten cents a head, children and niggers free — and business a growin' all the time; when somehow or another a little report got around, last night, that I had a way of puttin' in my time with a private jug, on the sly. A nigger rousted me out this mornin', and told me the people was gatherin' on the quiet, with their dogs and horses, and they'd be along pretty soon and give me 'bout half an hour's start, and then run me down, if they could; and if they got me they'd tar and feather me and ride me on a rail, sure. I didn't wait for no breakfast — I warn't hungry."

"Old man," says the young one. "I reckon we might double-team it together; what to you think?"

"I ain't undisposed. What's your line — mainly?"

"Do a little in patent medicines; theatre-actor — tragedy, you know; take a turn at mesmerism and phrenology when there's a chance; teach singing, geography, school for a change; sling a lecture, sometimes — oh, I do lots of things — most anything that comes handy, so it ain't work. What's your lay?"

"I've done considerable in the doctoring way in my time. Layin' on o' hands is my best holt — for cancer, and paralysis, and sich things; and I k'n tell a fortune pretty good, when I've got somebody along to find out the facts for me. Preachin's my line, too; and workin' camp-meetin's; and missionaryin' around.

Nobody never said anything for a while; then the young man hove a sigh and says:

"Alas !"

"What're you alassin' about?" says the baldhead.

"Ah, you would not believe me; the world never believes — let it pass — 'tis no matter. The secret of my birth —"

"The secret of your birth? Do you mean to say —"

"Gentlemen", says the young man, very solemn, "I will reveal it to you, for I feel I may have confidence in you. By rights I am a duke !"

Jim's eyes bugged out when he heard that; and I reckon mine did, too. Then the baldhead says: "No! you can't mean it?"

"Yes. My great-grandfather, eldest son of the Duke of Bridgewater, fled to this country about the end of the last century, to breathe the pure air of freedom; married here, and died, leaving a son, his own father dying about the same time. The second son of the late duke seized the title and estates — the infant real duke was ignored. I am the lineal descendant of that infant — I am the rightful Duke of Bridgewater."

Jim pitied him ever so much, and so did I. We tried to comfort him, but he said it warn't much use, he couldn't be much comforted; said if we was a mind to acknowledge him, that would do him more good than most anything else; so we said we would, if he would tell us how. He said we ought to bow, when we spoke to him, and say "Your Grace," or "My Lord," or "Your Lordship" — and one of us ought to wait on him at dinner, and do any little thing for him he wanted done.

Well, that was all easy, so we done it. All through dinner, Jim stood around and waited on him, and says, "Will yo' Grace have some o' dis, or some o' dat?" and so on, and a body could see it was mighty pleasing to him.

But the old man got pretty silent, by-and-by — didn't have much to say, and didn't look pretty comfortable over all that petting that was going around that duke. He seemed to have something on his mind. So, along in the afternoon, he says:

"Looky here, Bilgewater," he says, "I'm 'nation sorry for you, but you ain't the only person that's had troubles like that."

"No?"

"No, you ain't the only person that's had a secret of his birth." And by jings, he begins to cry.

"Hold! What do you mean?"

"Bilgewater, I am the late Dauphin!"

You bet you Jim and me stared, this time. Then the Duke says: ,,You are what?"

"Yes, my fried, it is too true — your eyes in lookin' at this very moment on the pore disappeared Dauphin, Looy the Seventeen, son of Looy the Sixteen and Marry Antonette. I should really be a King."

"You! At your age! No! You mean you're the late Charlemagne; you must be six or seven hundred years old, at the very least."

"Trouble has done it, Bilgewater, trouble has done it," said the king, solemn-like.

Come nightfall, we pushed off again. When we was three-quarters of a mile down river, we hoisted up our signal lantern; and about ten o'clock it come on to rain and blow and thunder and lighten like everything; so the king told us to both stay on watch till the weather got better; then him and the duke crawled into the wigwam and turned in for the night. In was my watch below, till twelve, but I wouldn't a turned in, anyway, if I'd had a bed; because a body don't see such a storm as that every day in the week, not by a long sight. The waves most washed me off the raft, sometimes, but I hadn't any clothes on, and didn't mind. We didn't have no trouble about snags; the lightning was glaring and flittering around so constant that we could see them plenty soon enough to throw her head this way or that and miss them.

I had the middle watch, you know, but I was pretty sleepy by that time, so Jim he said he would stand the first half of it for me; he was always mighty good that way, Jim was. I crawled into the wigwam, but the king and the duke had their legs sprawled around so there warn't no show for me; so I laid outside — I didn't mind the rain, because it was warm, and the waves warn't running so high now.

Then I took the watch, and Jim he laid down and snored away, and by-and-by the storm let up for good and all; and the first cabin-light that showed, I rousted him out and we slid the raft into hiding-quarters for the day.

The king got out an old ratty deck of cards, after breakfast, and him and the duke played seven-up a while, five cents a game. Then they got tired of it, and allowed they would "lay out a campaign," as they called it. The duke went down into his carpet-bag and fetched up a lot of little printed bills, and read them out loud. One bill said "The celebrated Dr. Armand de Montalban, of Paris," would "lecture on the Science of Phrenology" at such and such a place, on the blank day of blank, at ten cents admission, and "furnish charts of character at twenty-five cents apiece."

The duke said that was him. In another bill he was the "World-renowned Shakespearean tragedian, Garrick the Younger, of Drury Lane, London." In other bills he had a lot of other names and done other wonderful things, like finding water and gold with a "divining rod," dissipating "witch-spells," and so on. By-and-by he says:

"But the histrionic muse is the darling. Have you ever trod the boards, Royalty?"

"No," says the king.

"You shall, then, before you're three days older, Fallen Grandeur," says the duke. "The first good town we come to, we'll hire a hall and do the sword-fight in Richard III and the balcony scene in Romeo and Juliet. How does that strike you?"

"I'm in, up to the hub, for anything that will pay, Bilge-water, but you see I don't know nothing about play actin', and hain't ever seen much of it. I was too small when pap used to have 'em at the palace. Do you reckon you can learn me?"

"Easy!"

"All right. I'm jist a-freezn' for something fresh, anyway. Less commence, right away."

So the duke he told him all about who Romeo was, and who Juliet was, and said he was used to being Romeo, so the king could be Juliet.

"But if Juliet's such a young girl, Duke, my peeled head and my white whiskers is going' to look uncommon odd on her, maybe."

"No, don't you worry — these country jakes won't ever think of that. Besides, you know, you'll be in costume, and that makes all the difference in the world; Juliet's in a balcony, enjoying the moonlight before she goes to bed, and she's got on her night-gown and her ruffled night-cap. Here are the costumes for the parts."

He got out two or three curtain-calico suits, which he said was meedyevil armour for Richard III and t'other chap, and a long white cotton night-shirt and a ruffled night-cap to match. The king was satisfied; so the duke got out his book and read the parts over in the most splendid spread-eagle way, prancing around and acting at the same time, to show how it had got to be done; then he give the book to the king and told him to get his part by heart.

There was a little one-horse town about three miles down the bend, and after dinner the duke allowed he would go down to the town. The king allowed he would go too, and see if he couldn't strike something. We was out of coffee, so Jim said I better go along with them in the canoe and get some.

When we got there, there warn't nobody stirring; streets empty, and perfectly dead and still, like Sunday. We found a sick nigger sunning himself in the back yard, and he said everybody that warn't too young or too sick or too old was gone to camp-meeting, about two mile back in the woods. The king got the directions, and allowed he'd go and work that camp-meeting for all it was worth, and I might go, too.

The duke said what he was after was a printing office. We found it; a little bit of a concern, up over a carpenter shop — carpenters and printers all gone to the meeting, and no doors locked. It was a dirty, littered-up place and had ink marks, and handbills with pictures of horses and runaway niggers on them, all over the walls. The duke shed his coat and said he was all right, now. So me and the king lit out for the camp-meeting.

We got there in about a half an hour, fairly dripping, for it was a most awful hot day. There was as much as a thousand people there, from twenty mile around. The woods was full of teams and wagons, hitched everywheres, feeding out of the wagon troughs and stomping to keep off the flies. There was sheds made out of poles and roofed over with branches, where they had lemonade and gingerbread to sell, and piles of water-melons and green corn and such-like truck.

The preaching was going on under the same kinds of sheds, only they was bigger and held crowds of people.

The first shed we come to, the preacher was lining out a hymn. He lined out two lines, everybody sung it, and it was kind of grand to hear it, there was so many of them and they done it in such a rousing way; then he lined out two more for them to sing — and so on. The people woke up more and more, and sung louder and louder; and towards the end some begun to groan, and some begun to shout. Then the preacher begun to preach; and begun in earnest, too; and went weaving first to one side of the platform and then the other, and then a leaning down over the front of it, with his arms and his body going all the time, and shouting his words out with all his might; and every now and then he could hold up his Bible and spread it open, and kind of pass it around this way and that, saying, "It's the brazen serpent in the wilderness! Look upon it and live!" And people would shout out, "Glory! — A-a-men!" And so he went on, and the people groaning and crying and saying amen.

Well, the first I knowed, the king got agoing; and next he went a-charging up on to the platform and the preacher he begged him to speak to the people, and he done it. He told them he was a pirate — been a pirate for thirty years, out in the Indian Ocean, and his crew was thinned out considerable, last spring, in a fight, and he was home now, to take out some fresh men, and thanks to goodness he'd been robbed last night, and put ashore off of a steamboat without a cent, and he was glad of it, it was the blessedest thing that ever happened to him, because he was a changed man now, and happy for the first time in his life; and poor as he was he was going to start right off and work his way back to the Indian Ocean and put in the rest of his life trying to turn the pirates into the true path; for he could do it better than anybody else, being acquainted with all the pirate crews in that ocean; and though it would take him a long time to get there, without money, he would get there anyway, and every time he convinced a pirate he would say to him, "Don't you thank me, don't you give me no credit, it all belongs to them dear people in Pokeville camp-meeting, natural brothers and benefactors of the race — and that dear preacher there, the truest friend a pirate ever had!"

And then he bursted into tears, and so did everybody. Then somebody sings out "Take up a collection for him, take up a collection!" Well, a half a dozen made a jump to do it, but somebody sings out, "Let him pass the hat around!" Then everybody said it, the preacher too.

So the king went all through the crowd with his hat, swabbing his eyes, and blessing the people and praising them and thanking them for being so good to the poor pirates away off there; and every little while the prettiest kind of girls, with the tears running down their cheeks, would up and ask him would he let them kiss him, for to remember him by; and he always done it; and some of them he hugged and kissed as many as five or six times — and he was invited to stay a week; and everybody wanted him to live in their houses, and said they'd think it was an honour; but he said as this was the last day of the camp-meeting he couldn't do no good, and besides he was in a sweat to get to the Indian Ocean right off and go to work on the pirates.

When we got back to the raft and he came to count up, he found he had collected eighty-seven dollars and seventy-five cents. And then he had fetched away a three-gallon jug of whisky too, that he found under a wagon when he was starting home through the woods. The king said, take it all around, it laid over any day he'd ever put in in the missionarying line. He said it warn't no use talking, heathens dont' amount to shucks, alongside of pirates, to work a camp-meeting with.

The duke was thinking he'd been doing pretty well, till the king come to show up, but after that he didn't think so so much. He showed us a little job he'd printed. It had a picture of runaway nigger, with a bundle on a stick, over his shoulder, and "$ 200 reward" under it. The reading was all about Jim, and just described him to a dot. It said he run away from St. Jacques' plantation, forty miles below New Orleans, last winter, and likely went north, and whoever would catch him and send him back, he could have the reward and expenses.

"Now," says the duke, "after to-night, we can run in the daytime if we want to. Whenever we see anybody coming, we can tie Jim hand and foot with a rope, and lay him in the wigwam and show this handbill and say we captured him up the river, and were too poor to travel on a steamboat, so we got this little raft on credit from our friends and are going down to get the reward. Handcuffs and chains would look still better on Jim, but it wouldn't go well with the story of us being so poor.

We all said the duke was pretty smart, and there couldn't be no trouble about running daytimes. We judged we could make miles enough that night, then we would boom right along, if we wanted to.

We laid low and kept still, and never shoved out till nearly ten o'clock; then we slid by, pretty wide away from the town, and didn't hoist our lantern till we was clear out of sight of it.

CHAPTER NINE

Shakesperean Revival

It was after sun-up now, but we went right on, and didn't tie up.

The king and the duke turned out, by-and-by, looking pretty rusty; but after they'd jumped overboard and took a swim, it chippered them up a good deal. After breakfast, the king he took a seat on a corner of the raft, and pulled off his boots and rolled up his britches, and let his legs dangle in the water, so as to be comfortable, and lit his pipe, and went to getting his Romeo and Juliet by heart. When he had got it pretty good, him and the duke began to practise it together. The duke had to learn him over and over again, how to say every speech; and he made him sigh, and put his hand on his heart, and after a while he said he done it pretty well; "only," he says, "you mustn't bellow out *Romeo!* that way, like a bull — you must say it soft, and sick, and languishy, so — Ro-o-o-meo! that is the idea; for Juliet's a dear sweet mere child of a girl, you know, and she don't bray like a jackass."

Well, the next they got out a couple of long swords that the duke made out of oak laths, and begun to practise the swordfight — the duke called himself Richard III; and the way they laid on, and pranced around the raft was grand to see. But by-and-by the king tripped and fell overboard, and after that they took a rest, and had a talk about all kinds of adventures they'd had in other times along the river.

After dinner, the duke says:

"Well, we'll want to make this a first class show, you know, so I guess we'll add a little more to it. We want a little something to answer encores with, anyway."

"What's Onkores, Bilgewater?"

The duke told him, and then says:

"I'll answer by doing the Highland fling or the sailor's hornpipe: and you — well, let me see — oh, I've got it — and you can do Hamlet's soliloquy."

"Hamlet's which?"

"Hamlet's soliloquy, you know; the most celebrated thing in Shakespeare. Ah, it's sublime, sublime!"

The first chance we got, the duke he had some show bills printed: and after that, for two or three days as we floated along, the raft was a most uncommon lively place, for three warn't nothing but sword fighting and rehearsing — as the duke called it — going on all the time. One morning, when we was pretty well down the State of Arkansaw, we come in sight of a little one-horse town in a big bend; so we tied up about three-quarters of a mile above it, in the mouth of a crick which was shut in like a tunnel by the cypress trees, and all of us but Jim took the canoe and went down there to see if there was any chance in that place for our show.

We struck it mighty lucky; there was going to be a circus there that afternoon, and the country people was already beginning to come in, in all kinds of old shackly wagons, and on horses. The circus would leave before night, so our show would have a pretty good chance. The duke he hired the court house, and we went around and stuck up our bills. They read like this:

Shakespearean Revival ! ! !

Wonderful Attraction !

For One Night Only !

The World renowned tragedians,

David Garrick the younger, of Drury Lane Theatre, London,

and

Edmund Kean the elder, of the Royal Haymarket Theatre, Whitechapel, Pudding Lane, Piccadilly, London,

and the Royal Continental Theatres, in their

Sublime Shakespearean Spectacle entitled

The Balcony Scene

in

Romeo and Juliet ! ! !

Romeo	Mr. Garrick
Juliet	Mr. Kean

Asisted by the whole strength of the company !

New costumes, new scenery, new appointments !

Also:

The thrilling, masterly, and blood-curdling

Broad-sword conflict

In Richard III ! ! !

Richard III	Mr. Garrick
Richmond	Mr. Kean

Also: (by special request)

Hamlet's Immortal Soliloquy ! !

By the Illustrious Kean !

Done by him 300 consecutive nights in Paris !

For One Night Only,

On account of imperative European engagements !

Admission 25 cents; children and servants — 10 cents.

Then we went loafing around the town. The stores and houses was most all old shackly dried-up frame concerns that hadn't ever been painted; they was set up three or four feet above ground on stilts, so as to be out of reach of the water when the river was overflowed.

All the stores was along one street. They had white-domestic awnings in front, and the country people hitched their horses to the awning-posts. There was empty dry-goods boxes under the awnings and loafers roosting on them all day long, whittling them with their Barlow knives; and chawing tobacco, and gaping and yawning and stretching — a mighty ornery lot.

All the streets and lanes was just mud, they warn't nothing else but mud — mud as black as tar, and nigh about a foot deep in some places; and two or three inches deep in all the places.

The hogs loafed and grunted around, everywheres. You'd see a muddy sow and a litter of pigs come lazying along the street and whollop herself right down in the way, where folks had to walk around her, and she'd stretch out and shut her eyes, and wave her ears, whilst the pigs was milking her, and look as happy as if she was on salary.

And pretty soon you'd hear a loafer sing out, "Hi! so boy! sick him, Tige!" and away the sow would go, squealing most horrible, with a dog or two swinging to each ear, and three or four dozen more a-coming; and then you would see all the loafers get up and watch the thing out of sight, and laugh at the fun and look grateful for the noise.

The nearer it got to noon that day, the thicker and thicker was the wagons and horses in the streets, and more coming all the time. Families fetched their dinners with them, from the country, and eat them in the wagons. There was considerable whisky-drinking going on, and I seen three fights. By-and-by somebody sings out:

"Here comes old Boggs! — in from the country for his little old monthly drunk — here he comes, boys!"

All the loafers looked glad — I reckoned they was used to having fun out of Boggs. One of them says:

"Wonder who he's a gwyne to chaw up this time. If he'd a chawed up all the men he's ben a gwyne to chaw up in the last twenty year, he'd have considerable reputation, now."

Boggs comes a-tearing along on his horse, whooping and yelling like an Injun.

He see me, and rode up and says:

"Whar'd you come f'm boy? You prepared to die?"

Then he rode on. I was scared; but a man says: "He don't mean nothing; he's always a carryin' on like that when he's drunk. He's the best-naturedest old fool in Arkansaw — never hurt nobody, drunk nor sober."

Boggs rode up before the biggest store in town and bent his head down so as he could see under the curtain of the awning, and yells:

"Come out here, Sherburn! Come out and meet the man you've swindled. You're the houn' I'm after, and I'm a gwyne to have you, too!"

And so he went on, calling Sherburn everything he could lay his tongue to, and the whole street packed with people listening and laughing and going on. By-and-by a proud-looking man about fifty-five — and he was a heap the best-dressed man it that town, too — steps out of the store, and the crowd drops back on each side to let him come. He says to Boggs, mighty ca'm and slow — he says: "I'm tired of this; but I'll endure it till one o'clock. Till one o'clock, mind — no longer. If you open your mouth against me only once, after that time, you can't travel so far but I will find you."

Everybody that could get a chance at him tried their best to coax him off of his horse, so that they could lock him up and get him sober; but it warn't no use — up the stree he would tear again, and give Sherburn another cussing. By-and-by somebody says:

"Go for his daughter! — quick, go for his daughter; sometimes he'll listen to her. If anybody can persuade him, she can."

So somebody started on a run. I walked down street a ways, and stopped. In about five or ten minutes, here comes Boggs again — but not on his horse. He was a-reeling across the street towards me, bareheaded, with a friend on both sides of him aholt of his arms and hurrying him along. He was quiet, and looked uneasy; and he warn't hanging back any, but was doing some of the hurrying himself. Somebody sings out:

"Boggs!"

I looked over there to see who said it, and it was that Colonel Sherburn. He was standing perfectly still in the street, and had a pistol raised in his right hand — not aiming it, but holding it out with the barrel tilted up towards the sky. The same second I see a young girl coming on the run, and two men with her. Boggs and the men turned round, to see who called him, and when they see the pistol the men jumped to one side, and the pistol barrel come down slow and steady to a level — both barrels cocked. Boggs throws up both of his hands, and says, "O Lord, don't shoot!" Bang! goes the first shot, and he staggers back, clawing at the air — bang! goes the second one, and he tumbles backwards onto the ground, heavy and solid, with his arms spread out. That young girl screamed out, and comes rushing, and down she throws herself on her father, crying and saying, ,,Oh, he's killed him, he's killed him!" The crowd closed up around them, and shouldered and jammed one another, with their necks stretched, trying to see, and people on the inside trying to shove them back, and shouting, "Back!, back! give him air, give him air!"

Colonel Sherburn he tossed his pistol onto the ground, and turned around on his heels and walked off.

Then they pulled his daughter away from him, screaming and crying, and took her off. She was about sixteen, and very sweet and gentle-looking, but awful pale and scared.

There was considerable jawing back, so I slid out, thinking maybe there was going to be trouble. The streets was full, and everybody was excited. Everybody that seen the shooting was telling how it happened, and there was a big crowd packed around each one of these fellows, stretching their necks and listening.

Well, by-and-by somebody said Sherburn ought to be ynched. In about a minute everybody was saying it; so away they went, mad and yelling, and snatching down every clothes-line they come to, to do the hanging with.

CHAPTER TEN
Attending the Circus

They swarmed up the street towards Sherburn's house a-whooping and yelling and raging like Injuns, and everything had to clear the way or get run over and tromped to mush, and it was awful to see. Children was heeling it ahead of the mob, screaming and trying to get out of the way; and every window along the road was full of women's heads, and there was nigger boys in every tree, and bucks and wenches looking over every fence; and as soon as the mob would get nearly to them they would break and skaddle back out of reach. Lots of the women and girls was crying and taking on, scared most to death.

They swarmed up in front of Sherburn's palings as thick as they could jam together, and you couldn't hear yourself think for the noise. It was a little twenty-foot yard. Some sung out, "Tear down the fence! Tear down the fence!" Then there was a racket of ripping and tearing and smashing, and down she goes, and the front wall of the crowd begins to roll in like a wave.

Just then Sherburn steps out on to the roof of his little front porch, with a double-barrel gun in his hand, and takes his stand, perfectly calm and deliberate, not saying a word. The racket stopped, and the wave sucked back.

Sherburn never said a word — just stood there, looking down. The stillness was awful creepy and uncomfortable. Sherburn run his eyes slow along the crowd; and wherever it struck, the people tried a little to outgaze him, but they couldn't; they dropped their eyes and looked sneaky. Then pretty soon Sherburn sort of laughed; not the pleasant kind, but the kind that makes you feel when like you are eating bread that's got sand in it.

Then he says, slow and scornful:

"The idea of you lynching anybody! It's amusing. The idea of you thinking you had pluck enough to lynch a *man*! Because you're brave enough to tar and feather poor friendless cast-out women that come along here, did that make you think you had grit enough to lay your hands on a *man*? Now leave —" tossing his gun up across his left arm and cocking it, when he says this.

The crowd washed back sudden, and then broke all apart and went tearing off every which way. I could a staid, if I'd a wanted to, but I didn't want to.

I went to the circus, and loafed around the back side till the watchman went by, and then dived in under the tent. I had my twenty-dollar gold piece and some other money, but I reckoned I better save it, because there ain't no telling how soon you are going to need it, away from home and amongst strangers, that way. You can't be too careful. I ain't opposed to spending money on circuses, when there ain't no other way, but there ain't no use in *wasting* it on them.

It was a real bully circus. It was the splendidest sight that ever was, when they all come riding in, two and two, a gentleman and lady, side by side, the men just in their drawers and undershirts and no shoes nor stirrups and their hands resting on their thighs easy and comfortable — there must a'been twenty of them — and every lady with a lovely complexion, and perfectly beautiful, and looking just like a gang of real sure-enough queens, and dressed in clothes that cost millions of dollars, and just littered with diamonds. It was a powerful fine sight; I never see anything so lovely. And then one by one they got up and stood, and went a-weaving around the ring so gentle and wavy and graceful, the men looking ever so tall and airy and straight, with their heads bobbing and skimming along, away up there under the tent-roof, and every lady's rose-leafy dress flapping soft and silky around her hips, and she looking like the most loveliest parasol.

Well, all through the circus they done the most astonishing things; and all the time that clown carried on so it most killed the people. The ring-master couldn't ever say a word to him but he was back at him quick as a wink with the funniest things a body ever said; and how he ever could think of so many of them, and so sudden and so pat, was what I couldn't noway understand. Why I couldn't a thought of them in a year.

I don't know; there may be bullier circuses than what that one was, but I never struck them yet. Anyways it was plenty good enough for me; and wherever I run across it, it can have all of my custom, every time.

Well, that night we had our show; but there warn't only about twelve people there; just enough to pay expenses. And they laughed all the time, and that made the duke mad; and everybody left, anyway, before the show was over, but one boy which was asleep. So the duke said these Arkansaw lunkheads couldn't come up to Shakespeare; what they wanted was low comedy — and maybe something ruther worse than low comedy, he reckoned. He said he could size their style. So next morning he got some big sheets of wrapping-paper and some black paint, and drawed off some handbills and stuck them up all over the village. The bills said:

AT THE COURT HOUSE!

For 3 nights only.

The World-renowned Tragedians

DAVID GARRICK THE YOUNGER

and

EDMUND KEAN THE ELDER!

Of the London and Continental

Theatres,

In their Thrilling Tragedy of

THE KING'S CAMELOPARD

or

THE ROYAL NONESUCH!!!

Admission 50 cents.

Then at the bottom was the biggest line of all, which said: LADIES AND CHILDREN NOT ADMITTED.

"There," says he, "if that line don't fetch them, I don't know Arkansaw!"

Well, all day him and the king was hard at it, rigging up a stage, and a curtain, and a row of candles for footlights; and that night the house was jam full of men in no time. When the place couldn't hold no more, the duke he quit tending door and went around the back way and come onto the stage and stood up before the curtain, and the next minute the king come a-prancing out on all fours, naked; and he was painted all over, ring-streaked-and-striped, all sorts of colours, as splendid as a rainbow. The people most killed themselves laughing; and when the king got done capering, and capered off behind the scenes, they roared and clapped and stormed and haw-hawed till he come back and done it over again; and after that, they made him do it another time. Well, it would a made a cow laugh to see the shines that old idiot cut.

Then the duke he lets the curtain down, and bows to the people, and says the great tragedy will be performed only two nights more, on accounts of pressing London engagements, where the seats is all sold already for it in Drury Lane; and then he makes them another bow, and says if he has succeeded in pleasing them and instructing them, he will be deeply obleeged if they will mention it to their friends and get them to come and see it.

Twenty people sings out:

"What, is it over? Is that *all*?"

The duke says "Yes". Then there was a fine time. Everybody sings out "Sold," and rose up mad, and was a-going for that stage and them tragedians. But a big fine-looking man jumps up on a bench, and shouts:

"Hold on! Just a word, gentlemen." They stopped to listen. "We are sold — mighty badly sold. But we don't want to be the laughing-stock of this whole town, I reckon, and never hear the last of this thing as long as we live. No. What we want, is to go out of here quiet, and talk this show up, and sell the rest of the town! Then we'll all be in the same boat. Ain't that sensible?" ("You bet it is! — the jedge is right!" everybody sings out.) "All right, then — not a word about any sell. Go along home, and advise everybody to come and see the tragedy".

Next day you couldn't hear nothing around that town but how splendid the show was. House was jammed again, that night, and we sold this crowd the same way. When me and the king and the duke got home to the raft, we all had a supper; and by-and-by, about midnight, they made Jim and me back her out and float her down the middle of the river and fetch her in and hide her about two mile below town.

The third night the house was crammed again — and they warn't new-comers, this time, but people that was at the show the other two nights. I stood by the duke at the door, and I see that every man that went in had his pockets bulging, or something muffled up under his coat — and I see it warn't no perfumery neither, not by a long sight. I smelt sickly eggs by the barrel, and rotten cabbages, and such things; and if I know the signs of a dead cat being around, and I bet I do, there was sixty-four of them went in. I shoved in there for a minute, but it was too various for me, I couldn's stand it. Well, when the place couldn't hold no more people, the duke he give a fellow a quarter and told him to tend door for him a minute, and then he started around for the stage door, I after him; but the minute we turned the corner and was in the dark, he says:

"Walk fast, now, till you get away from the houses, and then shin for the raft like the dickens was after you!"

I done it, and he done the same. We struck the raft at the same time, and in less than two seconds we was gliding down stream, all dark and still, and edging towards the middle of the river, nobody saying a word. I reckoned the poor king was in for a gaudy time of it with the audience; but nothing of the sort; pretty soon he crawls out from the wigwam, and says:

"Well, how'd the old thing pan out this time, Duke?"

He hadn't been up town at all.

We never showed a light till we was about ten mile below that village. Then we lit up and had a supper, and the king and the duke fairly laughed their bones loose over the way they'd served them people.

Them rapscallions took in four hundred and sixty-five dollars in that three nights. I never see money hauled in by the wagon-load like that before.

CHAPTER ELEVEN

Information

Next day, towards night, we laid up under a little willow tow-head out in the middle, where there was a village on each side of the river, and the duke and the king begun to lay out a plan for working them towns. Jim he spoke to the duke, and said he hoped it wouldn't take but a few hours, because it got mighty heavy and tiresome to him when he had to lay all day in the wigwam tied with the rope. You see, when we left him all alone we had to tie him, because if anybody happened on him all by himself and not tied, it wouldn't look much like he was a runaway nigger, you know. So the duke said it was kind of hard to have to lay roped up all day, and he'd cipher out some way to get around it.

He was uncommon bright, the duke was, and he soon struck it. He dressed Jim up in King Lear's outfit — it was a long curtain calico gown, and a white horse-hair wig and whiskers; and then he took his theatre-paint and painted Jim's face and hands and ears and neck all over a dead dull solid blue, like a man that's been drownded nine days. Blamed if he warn't the horriblest looking outrage I ever see. Then the duke took and wrote out a sign on a shingle so:

Sick Arab — but harmless when not out of his head.

And he nailed that shingle to a lath, and stood the lath up four or five feet in front of the wigwam, Jim was satisfied. He said it was a sight better than laying tied a couple of years every day and trembling all over every time there was a sound. The duke told him to make himself free and easy, and if anybody ever come meddling around, he must hop out of the wigwam, and carry on a little, and fetch a howl or two like a wild beast, and he reckoned they would light out and leave him alone.

These rapscallions wanted to try the Nonesuch again, because there was so much money in it, but they judged it wouldn't be safe, because maybe the news might a worked along by this time. They couldn't hit no project that suited, exactly; so at last the duke said he reckoned he'd lay off and work his brains an hour or two and see if he couldn't put something on the Arkansaw village; and the king he allowed he would drop over to t'other village, without any plan, but just trust in Providence to lead him the profitable way — meaning the devil, I reckon. We had all bought store clothes where we stopped last; and now the king put his'n on, and he told me to put mine on. I done it, of course. The king's duds was all black, and he did look real swell and starchy. Jim cleaned up the canoe, and I got my paddle ready. There was a big steamboat laying at the shore away up under the point, about three mile above town — been there a couple of hours, taking on freight. Says the king:

"Seein' how I'm dressed, I reckon maybe I better arrive down from St. Louis, or Cincinnati, or some other big place. Go for the steamboat, Huckleberry; we'll come down to the village on her."

I didn't have to be ordered twice, to go and take a steamboat ride. I fetched the shore a half a mile above the village, and then went scooting along the bluff bank in the easy water. Pretty soon we come to a nice innocent-looking young country jake setting on a log swabbing the sweat off of his face, for it was powerful warm weather; and he had a couple of big carpet-bags by him.

"Wher' you bound for, young man?"

"For the steamboat; going to Orleans."

"Git aboard," says the king . "Hold on a minute, my servant'll he'p you with them bags. Jump out and he'p the gentleman, Adolphus" — meaning me, I see.

I done so, and then we all three started on again.

The young chap was mighty thankful; said it was tough work toting his baggage such weather. He asked the king where he was going, and the king told him he'd come down the river and landed at the other village this morning, and now he was going up a few mile to see an old friend on a farm up there. The young fellow says:

"When I first see you, I says to myself. "It's Mr. Wilks, sure, and he come mighty near getting here in time.' But then I says again, 'No, I reckon it ain't him, or else he wouldn't be paddling up the river.' You *ain*'t him, are you?"

"No, my name's Blodgett — Elexander Blodgett — Reverend Elexander Blodgett, I s'pose I must say, as I'm one o' the Lord's poor servants. But still I'm jist as able to be sorry for Mr. Wilks for not arriving in time, all the same, if he's missed anything by it — which I hope he hasn't."

"Well, he don't miss any property by it, because he'll get that all right; but he's missed seeing his brother Peter die — which he mayn't mind, nobody can tell as to that — but his brother would a give anything in this world to see *him* before he died; never talked about nothing else all these three weeks; hadn't seen him since they was boys together — and hadn't ever seen his brother William at all — that's the deef and dumb one — William ain't more than thirty or thirty-five. Peter and George was the only ones that come out here; George was the married brother; him and his wife both died last year. Harvey and William's the only ones that's left now; and, as I was saying, they haven't got here in time."

"Did anybody send 'em word?"

"Oh, yes; a month or two ago, when Peter was first took; because Peter said then that he sorter felt like he warn't going to get well this time. You see, he was pretty old, and George's g'yirls was too young to be much company for him, except Mary Jane the red-headed one; and so he was kinder lonesome after George and his wife died, and didn't seem to care much to live. He most desperately wanted to see Harvey — and William, too, for that matter — because he was one of them kind that can't bear to make a will. He left a letter behind for Harvey, and said he's told in it where his money was hid, and how he wanted the rest of the pro-perty divided up so George's g'yirls would be all right — for George didn't leave nothing. And that letter was all they could get him to put a pen to."

"Why do you reckon Harvey don't come? Wher' does he live?"

"Oh, he lives in England — Sheffield — preaches there — hasn't ever been in this country. He hasn't had any too much time — and besides he mightn't a got the letter at all, you know."

"Too bad, too bad he couldn't a lived to see his brothers, poor soul. You going to Orleans, you say?"

"Yes, but that ain't only a part of it. I'm going in a ship, next Wednesday, for Ryo Janeero, where my uncle lives."

"It's a pretty long journey. But it'll be lovely; I wisht I was agoing. Is Mary Jane the eldest? How old is the others?"

"Mary Jane's nineteen, Susan's fifteen, and Joanna's about fourteen — that's the one that gives herself to good works and has a hare lip."

"Poor things! To be left alone in the cold world so."

"Well, they could be worse off. Old Peter had friends and they ain't going to let them come to no harm. There's Hobson, the Babtis' preacher; and Deacon Lot Hovey, and Ben Rucker, and Abner Shackleford, and Levi Bell, the lawyer; and Dr. Robinson, and their wives, and the widow Bartley, and — well, there's a lot of them; but these are the ones that Peter was thickest with, and used to write about sometimes, when he wrote home; so Harvey'll know where to look for friends when he gets here."

Well, the old man he went on asking questions till he just fairly emptied that young fellow. Blamed if he didn't inquire about everybody and everything in that blessed town, and all about all the Wilkses; and about Peter's business — which was a tanner; and about George's — which was a carpenter; and about Harvey's — which was a dissentering minister; and so on, and so on. Then he says:

"What did you want to walk all the way up to the steamboat for?"

84

"Because she's a big Orleans boat, and I was afeard she mightn't stop there. When they're deep they won't stop for a hail. A Cincinnati boat will, but this is a St. Louis one."

"Was Peter Wilks well off?"

"Oh, yes, pretty well off. He had houses and land, and it's reckoned he left three or four thousand in cash hid up som'ers."

"When did you say he died?"

"I didn't say, but it was last night."

"Funeral tomorrow, likely?"

"Yes, 'bout the middle of the day."

"Well, it's all terrible sad; but we've all got to go, one time or another. So what we want to do is to be prepared; then we're all right."

"Yes, sir, it's the best way. Ma used to always say that."

When we struck the boat, she was about done loading, and pretty soon she got off. The king never said nothing about going aboard, so I lost my ride, after all. When the boat was gone, the king made me paddle up another mile to a lonesome place, then he got ashore, and says:

"Now hustle back, right off, and fetch the duke up here, and the new carpet-bags. And if he's gone over to t'other side, go over there and git him. And tell him to git himself up regardless. Shove along, now."

I see what he was up to; but I never said nothing, of course. When I got back with the duke, we hid the canoe and then they set down on a log, and the king told him everything, just like the young fellow had said it — every last word of it. And all the time he was a doing it, he tried to talk like an Englishman; and he done it pretty well, too, for a slouch. I can't imitate him, and so I ain't agoing to try to; but he really done it pretty good. Then he says: "How are you on the deef and dumb, Bilgewater?"

The duke said, leave him alone for that; said he had played a deaf and dumb person on the histrionic boards. So then they waited for a steamboat.

About the middle of the afternoon a couple of little boats come along, but they didn't come from high enough up the river; but at last there was a big one, and they hailed her. She sent out her yawl, and we went abord, and she was from Cincinnati; and when they found we only wanted to go four or five miles, they was booming mad, and give us a cussing, and said they wouldn't land us. But the king was calm. He says:

"If gentlemen kin afford to pay a dollar a mile apiece, to be took on and put off in a yawl, a steamboat kin afford to carry 'em, can't it?"

So they softened down and said it was all right; and when we got to the village, they yawled us ashore. About two dozen men flocked down, when they see the yawl a coming; and when the king says:

"Kin any of you gentlemen tell me where' Mr. Peter Wilks lives?" they give a glance at one another, and nodded their heads, as much as to say, "What d' I tell you?" Then one of them says, kind of soft and gentle:

"I'm sorry, sir, but the best we can do is to tell you where he did live yesterday evening."

Sudden as winking, the ornery old cretur went all to smash, and fell up against the man, and put his chin on his shoulders, and cried down his back, and says:

,,Alas, alas! our poor brother — gone, and we never got to see him; oh, it's too, too hard!"

Then he turns around blubbering, and makes a lot of idiotic signs to the duke on his hands, and blamed if he didn't drop a carpet-bag and bust out a-crying. If they warn't the beatenest lot, them two frauds, that ever I struck.

Well, the men gathered around, and sympathized with them, and said all sorts of kind things to them, and carried their carpet-bags up the hill for them, and let them lean on them and cry, and told the king all about his brother's last moments, and the king he told it all over again on his hands to the duke, and both of them took on about that dead tanner like the'd lost the twelve disciples. It was enough to make a body ashamed of the human race.

CHAPTER TWELVE

Funeral Orgies

The news was all over town in two minutes, and you could see the people tearing down on the run, from every which way, some of them putting on their coats as they come. Pretty soon we was in the middle of a crowd, and the noise of the tramping was like a soldier-march. The windows and door-yards was full; and every minute somebody would say, over a fence:

,,Is it *them*?"

And somebody trotting along with the gang would answer back and say:

,,You bet it is."

When we got to the house, the street in front of it was packed, and the three girls was standing in the door. Mary Jane was red-headed, but that don't make no difference, she was most awful beautiful, and her face and her eyes was all lit up like glory, she was so glad her uncles had come. The king he spread his arms, and Mary Jane she jumped for them, and the hare-lip jumped for the duke, and there they *had* it. Everybody most, leastways women, cried for joy to see them meet again at last and have such good times.

Then the king he hunched the duke, private — I see him do it — and then he looked around and see the coffin, over in the corner on two chairs; so then, him and the duke, and a hand across each other's shoulder, and t'other hand to their eyes, walked slow and solemn over there, everybody dropping back to give them room, and all the talk and noise stopped, people saying "Sh!" and all the men taking their hats off and dropping their heads, so you could a heard a pin fall. And when they got there, they bent over and looked in the coffin, and took one sight, and then they bust out a crying so you could a heard them to Orleans, most; and then they put their arms around each other's necks, and hung their chins over each other's shoulders; and then for three minutes, or maybe four, I never see two men leak the way they done. And mind you, everybody was doing the same; and the place was that damp I never see anything like it. Then one of them got on one side of the coffin, and t'other on t'other side, and they kneeled down and rested their foreheads on the coffin, and let on to pray all to theirselves. Well, when it come to that, it worked the crowd like you never see anything like it, and so everybody broke down and went to sobbing right out loud — the poor girls, too; and every woman, nearly, went up to the girls, without saying a word, and kissed them, solemn, on the forehead, and then put their hand on their head, and looked up towards the sky, with the tears running down, and then busted out and went off sobbing and swabbing, and give the next woman a show. I never see anything so disgusting.

Well, by-and-by the king gets up and comes forward a little, and works himself up and slobbers out a speech, all full of tears and flapdoodle about its being a sore trial for him and his poor brother to lose the diseased, and to miss seeing diseased alive, after the long journey of four thousand mile, but it's a trial that's sweetened and sanctified to us by this dear sympathy and those holy tears, and so he thanks them out of his heart and out of his brother's heart, because out of their mouths they can't, words being too weak and cold, and all that kind of rot and slush, till it was just sickening; and then he blubbers out a pious goody-goody Amen, and turns himself loose and goes to crying fit to bust.

And the minute the words was out of his mouth somebody over in the crowd struck up the doxolojer, and everybody joined in with all their might, and it just warmed you up and made you feel as good as church letting out. Music is a good thing; and after all that soul-butter and hogwash, I never see it freshen up things so, and sound so honest and bully.

Then the king begins to work his jaw again, and says how him and his nieces would be glad if a few of the main principal friends of the family would take supper here with them this evening, and help set up with the ashes of the diseased; and says if his poor brother laying yonder could speak, he knows who he would name, for they was names that was very dear to him, and mentioned often in his letters; and so he will name the same, to-wit, as follows, Rucker, and Abner Shackleford, and Levi Bell, and Dr. Robinson, and their wives, and the widow Bartley.

Rev. Hobson and Dr. Robinson was down to the end of the town, a-hunting together; that is, I mean the doctor was shipping a sick man to t'other world, and the preacher was pinting him right. Lawyer Bell was away up to Louisville on some business. But the rest was on hand, and so they all come and shook hands with the king and thanked him and talked to him; and then they shook hands with the duke, and didn't say nothing but just kept a-smiling and bobbing their heads like a passel of sapheads whilst he made all sorts of signs with his hands and said "Goo-goo — goo-goo-goo," all the time, like a baby that can't talk.

So the king he blatted along, and managed to inquire about pretty much everybody and dog in town, by his name, and mentioned all sorts of little things that happened one time or another in the town, or to George's family, or to Peter; and he always let on that Peter wrote him the things, but that was a lie, he got every blessed one of them out of that young flathead that we canoed up to the steamboat.

Then Mary Jane she fetched the letter her father left behind, and the king he read it out loud and cried over it. It give the dwelling-house and three thousand dollars, gold, to the girls; and it give the tanyard (which was doing a good business), along with some other houses and land (worth about seven thousand), and three thousand dollars in gold to Harvey and William, and told where the six thousand cash was hid, down cellar. So these two frauds said they'd go and fetch it up, and have everything square and above board; and told me to come with a candle. We shut the cellar door behind us, and when they found the bag they spilt it out on the floor, and it was a lovely sight, all them yaller-boys. My, the way the king's eyes did shine!

He slaps the duke on the shoulder and says:

"Oh, *this* ain't bully, nor noth'n! Oh, no, I reckon not! Why, Biljy, it beats the Nonesuch, *don't* it?"

The duke allowed it did. They pawed the yaller-boys, and sifted them through their fingers and let them jingle down on the floor; and the king says:

"It ain't no use talkin; bein' brothers to a rich dead man, and representatives of furrin heirs that's got left, is the line for you and me, Bilge. Thish-yer comes of trust'n to Providence. It's the best way, in the long run. I've tried 'em all, and ther' ain't no better way."

Most everybody would a been satisfied with the pile, and took it on trust; but no, they must count it. So they counts it, and it comes out four hundred and fifteen dollars short. Says the king:

"Dern him, I wonder what he done with that four hundred and fifteen dollars?"

They worried over that a while, and ransacked all around for it. Then the duke says:

"Well, he was a pretty sick man, and likely he made a mistake — I reckon that's the way of it. The best way's to let it go, and keep still about it. We can spare it."

"Oh shucks, yes, we can *spare* it. I don't k'yer noth'n 'bout that — it's the *count* I'm thinkin' about. We want to be awful square and open and above-board, here, you know. We want to lug this h'yer money upstairs and count it before everybody — then ther' ain't noth'n suspicious. But when the dead man says ther's six thous'n dollars, you know, we don't want to —"

"Hold on" says the duke. "Less make up the deffisit" — and he begun to haul out yaller-boys out of his pocket.

"It's a most amaz'n good idea, Duke — you *have* got a rattlin' clever head on you," says the king. "Blest it the old Nonesuch ain't a heppin' us out agin" — and he begun to haul out yallerjackets and stack them up.

I most busted them, but they made up the six thousand clean and clear.

"Say," says he duke, "I got another idea. Le's go upstairs and count this money, and then take and *give it to the girls.*"

"Good land, Duke, lemme hug you! It's the most dazzling idea 'at ever a man struck. You have cert'nly got the most astonishin' head I ever see. Oh, this is the boss dodge, ther' ain't no mistake 'bout it. Let 'em fetch along their suspicions now, if they want to — this'll lay'em out."

When we got upstairs, everybody gathered around the table, and the king he counted it and stacked it up, three hundred dollars in a pile — twenty elegant little piles; everybody looked hungry at it, and licked their chops. Then they raked it into the bag again, and I see the king begin to swell himself up for another speech. He says:

"Friends all, my poor brother that lays yonder has done generous by them that's left behind in the vale of sorrers. He has done generous by these-yer poor little lambs that he loved and sheltered, and that's left fatherless and motherless. Yes, and we that knowed him, knows that he would a done more generous by'em if he hadn't ben afeard o' woundin' his dear William and me. *Now, wouldn't* he? Ther' ain't no question 'bout it, in my mind. Well, then — what kind o' brothers would it be' that'd stand in his way at sech a time? And what kind o' uncles would it be that'd rob — yes, *rob* — sech poor sweet lambs as these 'at he loved so, at sech a time? If I know William — and I *think* I do — he — well, I'll jest ask him." He turns around and begins to make a lot of signs to the duke with his hands; and the duks he looks at him stupid and leather-headed a while, then all of a sudden he seems to catch his meaning, and jumps for the king, goo-gooing with all his might for joy, and hugs him about fifteen times before he lets up. Then the king says, ,,I knowed it; I reckon *that'll* convince anybody the way he feels about it. Here, Mary Jane, Susan, Joanner, take the money — take it *all*. It's the gift of him that lays yonder, cold but joyful."

Mary Jane she went for him, Susan and the hare-lip went for the duke, and then such another hugging and kissing I never see yet. And everybody crowded up with the tears in their eyes, and most shook the hands off of them frauds, saying all the time:

,,You *dear* good souls! — how *lovely!* — how *could* you!"

Well, then, pretty soon all hands got to talking about the diseased again, and how good he was, and what a loss he was, and all that; and before long a big iron-jawed man worked himself in there from outside, and stood a listening and looking, and not saying anything; and nobody saying anything to him either, because the king was talking and they was all busy listening. The king was saying — in the middle of something he'd started in on — ,, — they bein' partickler friends o' the diseased. That's why they're invited here this evenin'; but tomorrow we want all to come — everybody; for he respected everybody, he liked everybody, and so it's fitten that his funeral orgies sh'd be public."

And so he went a-mooning on and on, liking to hear himself talk, and every little while he fetched in his funeral orgies again, till the duke he couldn't stand it no more; so he writes on a little scrap of paper, ,,Obsequies, you old fool," and folds it up and goes to goo-gooing and reaching it over people's heads to him. The king he reads it, and puts it in his pocket, and says:

"Poor William, afflicted as he is, his *heart's* aluz right. Asks me to invite everybody to come to the funeral — wants me to make 'em all welcome. But he needn't a worried — it was jest what I was at."

Then he weaves along again, perfectly calm, and goes to dropping in his funeral orgies again every now and then, just like he done before. And when he done it the third time, he says:

"I say orgies, not because it's the common term, because it ain't obsequies bein' the common term — but because orgies is the right term. Obsequies ain't used in England no more, now — it's gone out. We say orgies now, in England. Orgies is better, because it means the thing you're after, more exact. It's a word that's made up out'n the Greek *orgo*, outside, open, abroad; and the Hebrew *jeesum*, to plant, cover up; hence *inter*. So, you see, funeral orgies is an open or public funeral."

He was the *worst* I ever struck. Well, the iron-jawed man he laughed right in his face. Everybody was shocked. Everybody says, "Why, *doctor!*" and Abner Shackleford says:

"Why, Robinson, hain't you heard the news? This is Harvey Wilks."

The king he smiled eager, and shoved out his flapper, and says: "Is it my poor brother's dear good friend and physician? I —"

"Keep your hands off of me!" says the doctor. "*You* talk like an Englishman — *don't* you? It's the worse imitation I ever heard. *You* Peter Wilks' brother! You're a fraud, that's what you are!"

Well, how they all took on! They crowded around the doctor, and tried to quiet him down, and tried to explain to him, and tell him Harvey'd showed in forty ways that he *was* Harvey, and knowed everybody by name, and the names of the very dogs, and begged and *begged* him not to hurt Harvey's feelings and the poor girls' feelings, and all that; but it warn't no use, he stormed right along, and said any man that pretended to be an Englishman and couldn't imitate the lingo no better than what he did, was a fraud and a liar. The poor girls was hanging to the king and crying; and all of a sudden the doctor ups and turns on *them*. He says:

"I was your father's friend, and I'm your friend; and I warn you *as* a friend, and an honest one, that wants to protect you and keep you out of harm and trouble, to turn your backs on that scoundrel, and have nothing to do with him, the ignorant tramp, with his idiotic Greek and Hebrew as he calls it. He is the thinnest kind of an impostor — has come here with a lot of empty names and facts which he has picked up somewheres, and you take them for *proofs*, and are helped to fool yourselves by these foolish friends here, who ought to know better. Mary Jane Wilks, you know me for your friend, and for your unselfish friend, too. Now listen to me: turn this pitiful rascal out — I *beg* you to do it. Will you?"

Mary Jane straightened herself up, and my, but she was handsome! She says:

"*Here* is my answer," She hove up the bag of money and put it in the king's hands, and says, "Take this six thousand dollars, and invest it for me and my sisters any way you want to and don't give us no receipt for it."

Then she put her arm around the king on the one side, and Susan and the hare-lip done the same on the other. Everybody clapped their hands and stomped on the floor like a perfect storm, whilst the king help up his head and smiled proud. The doctor says:

"All right, I wash *my* hands of the matter. But I warn you all that a time's coming when you're going to feel sick whenever you think of this day" — and away he went.

"All right, doctor," says the king, kinder mocking him, "we'll try and get 'em to send for you" — which made them all laugh, and they said it was a prime good hit.

CHAPTER THIRTEEN

Question Time

Well, when they was all gone, the king he asks Mary Jane how they was off for spare rooms, and she said she had one spare room, which would do for Uncle William, and she'd give her own room to Uncle Harvey, which was a little bigger, and she would turn into the room with her sisters and sleep on a cot: and up in the garret was a little cubby, with a pallet in it. The king said the cubby would do for his valley — meaning me.

So Mary Jane took us up, and she showed them their rooms, which was plain but nice. The duke's room was pretty small, but plenty good enough, ans so was my cubby.

That night they had a big supper, and all them men and women was there, and I stood behind the king and the duke's chairs and waited on them, and the niggers waited on the rest. And when it was all done, me and the hare-lip had supper in the kitchen off of the leavings, whilst the others was helping the niggers clean up the things. The hare-lip she got to pumping me about England, and blest if I didn't think the ice was getting mighty thin, sometimes. She says:

"Did you ever see the king?"

"Who? William Fourth? Well, I bet I have — he goes to our church." I knowed he was dead years ago, but I never let on. So when I say he goes to our church, she says:

"What — regular?"

"Yes — regular. His pew's right over opposite ourn — on t'other side the pulpit."

"I thought he lived in London?"

"Well, he does. Where *would* he live?"

"But I thought *you* lived in Sheffield?"

I see I was up a stump. I had to let on to get choked with a chicken bone, so as to get time to think how to get down again.

Then she says:

"How is servants treated in England? Do they treat 'em better'n we treat our niggers?"

"No! A servant ain't nobody there. They treat them worse than dogs."

"Don't they give 'em holidays, the way we do, Christmas and New Year's week, and Fourth of July?"

"Oh, just listen! A body could tell *you* hain't ever been to England, by that. Why Hare-l — why, Joanna, they never see a holiday from year's end to year's end; never go to the circus, nor theatre, nor nigger shows, nor nowheres."

"Nor church?"

"Nor church."

"But *you* always went to church?"

Well, I was up again. I forgot I was the old man's servant. But next minute I whirled in on   kind of an explanation how a valley was different from a common servant, and *had* to go to church whether he wanted to or not, and set with the family, on account of its being the law. But I didn't do it pretty good, and when I got done I see she warn't satisfied. She says:

"Honest Injun, now, hain't you been telling me a lot of lies?"

"Honest Injun," says I.

"None of it at all?"

"None of it at all. Not a lie in it," says I.

"Lay your hand on this book and say it."

I see it warn't nothing but a dictionary, so I laid my hand on it and said it. So then she looked a little better satisfied, and says:

"Well, then, I'll believe some of it; but I hope to gracious if I'll believe the rest."

"What is it you won't believe, Joe?" says Mary Jane, stepping in with Susan behind her. ,,It ain't right nor kind for you to talk so to him, and him a stranger and so far from his people. How would you like to be treated so?"

"That's always your way, Maim — always sailing in to help somebody before they're hurt. I hain't done nothing to him. He's told some stretchers, I reckon; and I said I wouldn't swallow it all; and that's every bit and grain I did say. I reckon he can stand a little think like that, can't he?"

"I don't care whether 'twas little or whether 'twas big, he's here in our house and a stranger, and it wasn't good of you to say it. If you was in his place, it would make you feel ashamed; and so you oughtn't to say a thing to another person that will make them feel ashamed."

"Why, Maim, he said —"

"It don't make no difference what he *said* — that ain't the thing. The thing is for you to treat him *kind*, and not be saying things to make him remember he ain't in his own country, and amongst his own folks."

I says to myself this is a girl that I'm letting that old reptile rob her of her money!

Then Susan *she* waltzed in; and if you'll believe me, she did give Hare-lip hark from the tomb!

I says to myself, this is *another* one that I'm letting him rob of her money. And when she got through, they all jest laid theirselves out to make me feel at home and know I was amongst friends. I felt so ornery and low down and mean, that I says to myself, My mind's made up; I'll hive that money for them or bust.

So then I lit out — for bed, I said, meaning some time or another. When I got by myself, I went to thinking the thing over. I says to myself, Shall I go to the doctor, private, and blow on these frauds? No — that won't do. He might tell who told him; then the king and the duke would make it warm for me. Shall I go, private, and tell Mary Jane? No — I dasn't do it. Her face would give them a hint, sure; they've got the money and they'd slide right out and get away with it. If she was to fetch in help, I'd get mixed up in the business, before it was done with, I judge. No, there ain't no good way but one. I got to steal that money, somehow; and I got to steal it some way that they won't suspicion that I done it. They've got a good thing, here; and they ain't a-going to leave till they've played this family and this town for all they're worth, so I'll find a chance time enough. I'll steal it, and hide it; and by-and-by, when I'm away down the river, I'll write a letter and tell Mary Jane where it's hid. But I'd better hive it tonight, if I can, because the doctor maybe hasn't let up as much as he lets on he has; he might scare them out of here, yet.

So, thinks I, I'll go and search them rooms. Upstairs the hall was dark, but I found the duke's room, and started to paw around it with my hands; but I recollected it wouldn't be much like the king to let anybody else take care of that money but his own self; so then I went to his room and begun to paw around there. But I see I couldn't do nothing without a candle, and I dasn't light one, of course. So I judged I'd got to do the other thing — lay for them, and eavesdrop. About that time, I hears their footsteps coming, and was going to skip under the bed; I reached for it, but it wasn't where I thought it would be; but I touched the curtain that hid Mary Jane's frocks, so I jumped in behind that and snuggled in amongst the gowns and stood there perfectly still.

They come in and shut the door; and the first thing the duke done was to get down and look under the bed. Then I was glad I hadn't found the bed when I wanted it. And yet, you know, it's kind of natural to hide under the bed when you are up to anything private. They sets down, then, and the king says:

"Well, this is it, Capet. I ain't easy; I ain't comfortable. That doctor lays on my mind. I wanted to know your plans. I've got a notion, and I think it's a sound one."

"What is it, Duke?"

"That we better glide out of this, before three in the morning, and clip it down the river with what we've got. Specially, seeing we got it so easy — *given* back to us, flung at our heads, as you may say, when of course we allowed to have to steal it back. I'm for knocking off and lighting out."

That made me feel pretty bad. About an hour or two ago, it would a been a little different, but now it made me feel bad and disappointed. The king rips out and says:

"What! And not steel out the rest o' the property? March off like a passel o' fools and leave eight or nine thous'n' dollars' worth o' property layin' around just sufferin' to be scooped in? — and all good salable stuff, too."

The duke he grumbled; said the bag of gold was enough and he didn't want to go no deeper — didn't want to rob a lot of orphans of *everything* they had.

"Why, how you talk!" says the king. ,,We shan't rob 'em of nothing at all but jest this money. The people that *buys* the property is the suff'rers; because as soon's it's found out 'at we didn't own it — which won't be long after we've slid — the sale won't be valid, and it'll all go back to the estate. These — yer orphans'll git their house back agin, and that's enough for *them;* they're young and spry, and k'n easy earn a livin'. *They* ain't a-going to suffer. Why, jest think — there's thous'n's and thous'n's that ain't nigh so well off. Bless you, they ain't got noth'n to complain of."

Well, the king he talked him blind; so at last he give in, and said all right, but said he believed it was blame foolishness to stay, and that doctor hanging over them. But the king says:

"Cuss the doctor! What do we k'yer for *him?* Hain't we got all the fools in town on our side? and ain't that a big enough majority in any town?"

100

So they got ready to go downstairs again. The duke says: "I don't think we put that money in a good place."

That cheered me up. I'd begin to think I warn't going to get a hint of no kind to help me. The king says: "Why?"

"Because Mary Jane'll be in mourning from this out; and first you know the nigger that does up the rooms will get an order to box these duds up and put 'em away; and do you reckon a nigger can run across money and not borrow some of it?"

"Your head's level, agin, Duke," says the king; and he come a fumbling under the curtain two or three feet from where I was. I stuck tight to the wall, and kept mighty still, though quivery; and I wondered what them fellows would say to me if they catched me; and I tried to think what I'd better do if they did catch me. But the king he got the bag before I could think more than about a half a thought, and he never suspicioned I was around. They took and shoved the bag through a rip in the straw tick that was under the feather bed, and crammed it in a foot or two amongst the straw and said it was all right, now, because a nigger only makes up the feather bed, and don't turn over the straw tick only about twice a year, and so it warn't in no danger of getting stole, now.

But I knowed better. I had it out of there before they was half-way downstairs. I groped along up to my cubby, and hid it there till I could get a chance to do better. I judged I better hide it outside of the house somewheres, because if they missed it they would give the house a good ransacking. I knowed that very well. Then I turned in, with my clothes all on; but I couldn't a gone to sleep, if I'd a wanted to, I was in such a sweat to get through with the business. By-and-by I heard the king and the duke come up; so I rolled off of my pallet and laid with my chin at the top of my ladder and waited to see if anything was going to happen. But nothing did.

So I held on till all the late sounds had quit and the early ones hadn't begun, yet; and then I slipped down the ladder.

CHAPTER FOURTEEN

The Funeral

I crept to their doors and listened; they was snoring, so I tiptoed along, and got downstairs all right. There warn't a sound anywheres. I peeped through a crack of the dining-room door, and see the men that was watching the corpse all sound asleep on their chairs. The door was open into the parlour, where the corpse was laying, and there was a candle in both rooms, I passed along, and the parlour door was open; but I see there warn't nobody in there but the remainders of Peter; so I shoved on by; but the front door was locked, and the key wasn't there. Just then I heard somebody coming down the stairs, back behind me. I run in the parlour, and took a swift look around, and the only place I see to hide the bag was in the coffin. The lid was shoved along about a foot, showing the dead man's face down in there, with a wet cloth over it, and his shroud on. I tucked the money bag in under the lid, just down beyond where his hands was crossed, which made me creep, they was so cold, and then I run back across the room and in behind the door.

The person coming was Mary Jane. She went to the coffin, very soft, and kneeled down and looked in; then she put up her handkerchief and I see she begun to cry, though I couldn't hear her, and her back was to me. I slid out, and as I passed the dining-room, I thought I'd make sure them watchers hadn't seen me; so I looked through the crack and everything was all right. They hadn't stirred.

I slipped up to bed, feeling rather blue, on accounts of the thing playing out that way after I had took so much trouble and run so much risk about it. Says I, if it could stay where it is, all right; because when we get down the river a hundred mile or two, I could write back to Mary Jane, and she could dig him up again and get it: but that ain't the thing that's going to happen; the thing that's going to happen is, the money'll be found when they come to screw on the lid. Then the king'll get it again, and it'll be a long day before he gives anybody another chance to smouch it from him. Of course I *wanted* to slide down and get it out of there, but I dasn't try it. Every minute it was getting earlier, now, and pretty soon some of them watchers would begin to stir, and I might get catched — catched with six thousand dollars in my hands that nobody hadn't hired me to take care of. I don't wish to be mixed up in no such business as that, I says to myself.

When I got downstairs in the morning the parlour was shut up, and the watchers was gone. There warn't nobody around but the family and the widow Bartley and our tribe. I watched their faces to see if anything had been happening, but I couldn't tell.

Towards the middle of the day the undertaker come, with his man, and they set the coffin in the middle of the room on a couple of chairs, and then set all our chairs in rows, and borrowed more from the neighbours till the hall and the parlour and the dining-room was full. I see the coffin lid was the way it was before, but I dasn't go to look in under it, with folks around.

Then the people begun to flock in, and the beats and the girls took seats in the front row at the head of the coffin, and for half an hour the people filed around slow, in single rank, and looked down at the dead man's face a minute, and some dropped in a tear, and it was all very still and solemn, only the girls and the beats holding handkerchiefs to their eyes and keeping their heads bent, and sobbing a little. There warn't no other sound but the scraping of the feet on the floor, and blowing noses — because people always blows them more at a funeral than they do at other places except church.

When the place was packed full, the undertaker he slid around in his black gloves with his softy soothering ways, putting on the last touches, and getting people and things all shipshape and comfortable, and making no more sound than a cat. He never spoke; he moved people around, he squeezed in late ones, he opened up passage-ways, and done it all with nods and signs with his hands. Then he took his place over against the wall. He was the softest, glidingest, stealthiest man I ever see; and there warn't no more smile to him than there is to a ham.

Well, the funeral sermon was very good, but pison long and tiresome; and then the king he shoved in and got off some of his usual rubbage, and at last the job was through and the undertaker begun to sneak up on the coffin with his screw-driver. I was in a sweat then, and watched him pretty keen. But he never meddled at all; just slid the lid along, as soft as mush, and screwed it down tight and fast. So there I was! I didn't know whether the money was in there, or not.

They buried him, and we come back home, and I went to watching faces again — I couldn't help it, and I couldn't rest easy. But nothing come of it; the faces didn't tell me nothing.

The king he visited around, in the evening, and sweetened everybody up, and made himself ever so friendly; and he give out the idea that his congregation over in England would be in a sweat about him, so he must hurry and settle up the estate right away, and leave for home. And he said of course him and William would take the girls home with them; and that pleased everybody too, because then the girls would be well fixed, and amongst their own relations; and it pleased the girls, too — tickled them so they clean forgot they ever had a trouble in the world; and told him to sell out as quick as he wanted to, they would be ready.

Well, blamed if the king didn't bill the house and the niggers and all the property for auction straight off — sale two days after the funeral; but everybody could buy private beforehand it they wanted to.

So the next day after the funeral, along about noon-time the girls' joy got the first jolt; a couple of nigger traders come along, and the king sold them the niggers reasonable, for three-day drafts as they called it, and away they went, the two sons up the river to Memphis, and their mother down the river to Orleans. I thought them poor girls and them niggers would break their hearts for grief; they cried around each other, and took on so it most made me down sick to see it. The girls said they hadn't ever dreamed of seeing the family separated or sold away from the town.

The thing made a big stir in the town, too, and a good many come out flat-footed and said it was scandalous to separate the mother and the children that way.

Next day was auction day. About broad-day in the morning, the king and the duke come up in the garret and woke me up, and I see by their look that there was trouble. The king says:

"Was you in my room night before last?"

"No, your Majesty," — which was the way I always called him when nobody but our gang warn't around.

"Was you in there yisterday er last night?"

"No, your Majesty."

The duke says:

"Have you seen anybody else go in there?"

"Well, I see the niggers go in there several times."

Both of them give a little jump; and looked like they hadn't ever expected it, and then like they *had*.

Then the duke says:

"What, *all* of them?"

"No — leastways not all at once. That is, I don't think I ever see them all come *out* at once but just one time."

"Well, go on, go on — what did they do? How'd they act?"

"They didn't do nothing. They didn't act anyway, much, as fur as I see. They tip-toed away; so I seen, easy enough, that they'd shoved in there to do up your majesty's room, or something, s'posing you was up; and found you *warn't* up, and so they was hoping to slide out of the way of trouble without waking you up, if they hadn't already waked you up."

"Great guns, *this is* a go!" says the king. Then he says to the duke: "We got to jest swaller it, and say noth'n; mum's the word for *us*."

As they was starting down the ladder, the duke he chuckles again and says:

"Quick sales *and* small profits! It's a good business — yes." The king snarls around on him and says:

"I was trying to do for the best, in sellin' 'm out so quick. If the profits has turned out to be none, lackin' considerable, and none to carry, is it my fault any more'n it's yourn?"

"Well, *they'd* be in this house yet, and we *wouldn't* if I could a got my advice listened to."

So they went off a jawing; and I felt dreadful glad I'd worked it all off onto the niggers, and yet hadn't done the niggers no harm by it.

CHAPTER FIFTEEN

Mary Jane's Decision

By-and-by it was getting-up time; so I come down the ladder and started for downstairs, but as I come to the girls room, the door was open, and I see Mary Jane setting by her old hair trunk, which was open and she'd been packing things in it — getting ready to go to England. But she had stopped now, with a folded gown in her lap, and had her face in her hands, acrying. I felt awful bad to see it; of course anybody would. I went in there, and says:

"Miss Mary Jane, you can't abear to see people in trouble, and I can't — most always. Tell me about it."

So she done it. And it was the niggers — I just expected it. She said the beautiful trip to England was most about spoiled for her, she didn't know how she was ever going to be happy there, knowing the mother and the children warn't ever going to see each other no more — and then busted out bitterer than ever, and flung up her hands, and says:

"Oh, dear, dear, to think they ain't *ever* going to see each other any more!"

"But they *will* — and inside of two weeks — and I *know* it!" says I.

Laws it was out before I could think! — and before I could budge she throws her arms around my neck, and told me to say it *again*, say it *again*, say it *again!*

I see I had spoke too sudden, and said too much, and was in a close place. I asked her to let me think a minute; and she set there, very impatient and excited, and handsome.

Well, I says to myself, at last, I'll up and tell the truth this time, though it does seem most like setting down on a kag of powder and touching it off just to see where you'll go to. Then I says:

"Miss Mary Jane, is there any place out of town a little ways, where you could go and stay three or four days?"

"Yes — Mr. Lothrop's. Why?"

"Never mind why, yet. If I'll tell you how I know the niggers will see each other again — inside of two weeks — here in this house — and *prove* how I know it — will you go to Mr. Lothrop's and stay four days?"

"Four days"! she says; "I'll stay a year!"

"All right," I says, "I don't want nothing more out of *you* than just your word — I druther have it than another man's kiss-the-Bible." She smiled, and reddened up very sweet, and I says, "if you don't mind it, I'll shut the door — and bolt it."

Then I come back and set down again, and says:

"These uncles of yourn ain't no uncles at all — they're a couple of frauds — regular dead-beats."

It jolted her up like everything, of course; but I was over the shoal water now, so I went right along, her eyes a blazing higher and higher all the time, and told her every blame thing, from where we first struck that young fool going up to the steamboat, clear through to where she flung herself onto the king's breast at the front door, and he kissed her sixteen or seventeen times — and then up she jumps, with her face afire like sunset, and says:

"You tell me what to do, and whatever you say, I'll do it."

"Well," I says, "it's a rough gang, them two frauds, and I'm fixed so I got to travel with them a while longer, whet her I want to or not — I'd be all right, but there'd be anot her

108

person that you don't know about who'd be in big trouble. Well, we got to save *him*, hain't we? Of course. Well, then, we won't blow on them."

Saying them words put a good idea in my head. I see how maybe I could get me and Jim rid of the frauds; get them jailed here, and then leave. But I didn't want to run the raft in day-time, so I didn't want the plan to begin working till pretty late tonight. I says: "Miss Mary Jane, I'll tell you what we'll do — and you won't have to stay at Mr. Lothrop's so long, nuther. How far is it?"

"A little short of four miles — right out in the country, back here."

"Well, that'll answer. Now you go along out there, and lay low till nine or half-past, tonight, and then get them to fetch you home again — tell them you've thought of something. If you get here before eleven, put a candle in this window, and if I don't turn up, wait till eleven, and then if I don't turn up it means I'm gone, and out of the way, and safe. Then you come out and spread the news around, and get these beasts jailed."

"Good," she says, "I'll do it."

"And if it just happens so that I don't get away, but get took up along with them, you must up and say I told you the whole thing beforehand, and you must stand by me all you can."

"Stand by you, indeed I will. They shan't touch a hair of your head!" she says, and I see her nostrils spread and her eyes snap when she said it, too.

I judged we had got everything fixed about right, now So I says: "Just let the auction go right along, and don't worry. Nobody don't have to pay for the things they buy till a whole day after the auction, on accounts of the short notice, and they ain't going out of this till they get that money — and the way we've fixed it, the sale ain't going to count, and they ain't going to get no money. It's just like the way it was with the niggers — it warn't no sale, and the niggers will be back before long. Why, they can't collect the money for the *niggers*, yet — they're in the worst kind of a fix, Miss Mary."

"Well," she says, "I'll run down to breakfast now, and then I'll start straight for Mr. Lothrop's."

"Deed, that ain't the ticket, Miss Mary Jane," I says, "by no manner of means; go before breakfast."

"Why?"

"What did you reckon I wanted you to go at all for, Miss Mary?"

"Well, I never thought — and come to think, I don't know. What was it?"

"Why, it's because you ain't one of these leather-face people. I don't want no better book than what your face is. A body can set down and read it off like coarse print. Do you reckon you can go and face your uncles, when they come to kiss you good-morning, and never —"

"There, there, don't! Yes, I'll go before breakfast — I'll be glad to. And leave my sisters with them?"

"Yes — never mind about them. They've got to stand it yet a while. They might suspicion something if all of you was to go. I don't want you to see them, nor your sisters, nor nobody in this town — if a neighbour was to ask how is your uncles this morning, your face would tell something. No, you go right along, Miss Mary Jane, and I'll fix it with all of them. I'll tell Miss Susan to give your love to your uncles and say you've went away for a few hours for to get a little rest and change, or to see a friend, and you'll be back tonight or early in the morning."

"Gone to see a friend is all right, but I won't have my love given to them."

"Well, then, it shan't be." It was well enough to tell *her* so — no harm in it. It was only a little thing to do, and no trouble; and it's the little things that smoothes people's roads the most, down here below; it would make Mary Jane comfortable, and it wouldn't cost nothing. Then I says: "There's one more thing — that bag of money".

"Well, they've got that; and it makes me feel pretty silly to think how they got it."

"No, you're out, there. They hain't got it."

"Why, who's got it?"

"I wish I knowed, but I don't. I *had* it, because I stole it from them: and I stole it to give to you; and I know where I hid it, but I'm afraid it ain't there no more. I'm awfully sorry, Miss Mary Jane, I'm just as sorry as I can be; but I done the best I could: I did, honest. I come nigh getting caught, and I had to shove it into the first place I come to, and run — and it warn't a good place."

"Oh stop blaming yourself — it's too bad to do it, and I won't allow it — you couldn't help it; it wasn't your fault. Where did you hide it?"

I didn't want to set her thinking about her troubles again; and I couldn't seem to get my mouth to tell her what would make her see that corpse lying in the coffin with that bag of money on his stomach. So for a minute I didn't say nothing — then I says:

"I'd rather not *tell* you where I put it, Miss Mary Jane, if you don't mind letting me off; but I'll write it for you on a piece of paper, and you can read it along the road to Mr. Lothrop's, if you want to. Do you reckon that'll do?"

"Oh, yes."

So I wrote: "I put it in the coffin. It was in there when you was crying there, away in the night. I was behind the door, and I was mighty sorry for you, Miss Mary Jane."

It made my eyes water a little, to remember her crying there all by herself at night, and them devils laying there right under her own roof, shaming her and robbing her; and when I folded it up and give it to her, I see the water come into her eyes, too; and she shook me by the hand, hard, and says:

"Good-bye — I'm going to do everything just as you've told me; and if I don't ever see you again I shan't ever forget you, and I'll think of you a many and a many a time, and I'll pray for you, too!" and she was gone.

Pray for me! I reckoned if she knowed me she'd take a job that was more nearer her size. But I bet she done it, just the same — she was just that kind. She had the grit to pray for Judas if she took the notion — there warn't no backdown to her, I judge. You may say what you want to, but in my opinion she was just full of sand. It sounds like flattery, but it ain't no flattery. And when it comes to beauty — and goodness too — she lays over them all. I hain't ever seen her since, but I reckon I've thought of her a many and a many a million times, and of her saying she would pray for me; and if I'd a thought it would do any good for me to pray for *her*, blamed if I wouldn't a done it or bust.

Well, Mary Jane she lit out the back way, I reckon; because nobody see her go. When I struck Susan and the hare-lip, I says:

"What's the name of them people over on t'other side of the river that you all goes to see sometimes?"

They says:

"There's several; but it's the Proctors, mainly."

"That's the name," I says; "I most forgot it. Well, Miss Mary Jane she told me to tell you she's gone over there in a dreadful hurry — one of them's sick."

"I reckon we ought to tell Uncle Harvey she's gone out a while, anyway, so he won't be uneasy about her?"

"Yes, Miss Mary Jane she wanted you to do that. She says, 'Tell them to give Uncle Harvey and William my love and a kiss.'"

"All right," they said, and cleared out to lay for their uncles, and give them the love and the kisses, and tell them the message.

Well, they held the auction in the public square, along towards the end of the afternoon, and it strung along and strung along, and the old man he was on hand and looking his level piousest, up there longside of the auctioneer, and chipping in a little Scripture, now and then, or a little goody-goody saying, of some kind, and the duke he was around goo-gooing for sympathy all he knowed how, and just spreading himself generly.

Well, whilst they was at it, a steamboat landed, and in about two minutes up comes a crowd a whooping and yelling and laughing and carrying on, and singing out:

"Here's your opposition line ! Here's your two set o' heirs to old Peter Wilks — and you pays your money and you takes your choice !"

They was fetching a very nice-looking old gentleman along, and a nice-looking younger one, with his right arm in a sling. And my souls, how the people yelled, and laughed, and kept it up. But I didn't see no joke about it, and I judged it would strain the duke and the king some to see any. I reckoned they'd turn pale. But no, nary a pale did *they* turn.

That old gentleman that had just come looked all puzzled to death. Pretty soon he begun to speak, and I see, straight off, he pronounced like an Englishman, not the king's way, though the king's was pretty good for an imitation.

"This is a surprise to me which I wasn't looking for; and I'll acknowledge, candid and frank, I ain't very well fixed to meet it and answer it; for my brother and me has had misfortunes, he's broke his arm, and our baggage got put off at a town above here, last night in the night by a mistake. I am Peter Wilks's brother Harvey, and this is his brother William, which can't hear nor speak — and can't even make signs to amount to much, now't he's only got one hand to work with. We are who we say we are ; and in a day or two, when I get the baggage, I can prove it. But, up till then, I won't say nothing more, but go to the hotel and wait."

So him and the new dummy started off; and the king he laughs, and blethers out:

"Broke his arm — *very* likely, ain't it? — and very convenient, too, for a fraud that's got to make signs, and hain't learnt how. Lost their baggage ! That's *mighty* good ! — and mighty ingenious — under the *circumstances !*"

So he laughed again; and so did everybody else, except three or four, or maybe a dozen. One of these was that doctor; another one was a sharp-looking gentleman, with a carpet-bag of the old-fashioned kind made out of carpet-stuff, that had just come off of the steambot and was talking to him in a low voice, and glancing towards the king now and then and nodding their heads — it was Levi Bell, the lawyer that was gone up to Louisville; and another one was a big rough husky that come along and listened to all the old gentleman said, and was listening to the king now. And when the king got done, this husky up and says:

"Say, looky here; if you are Harvey Wilks, when'd you come to this town?"

"The day before the funeral, friend," says the king.

"But what time o'day?"

"In the evenin' — 'bout an hour er two before sundown."

"*How'd* you come?"

"I come down on the *Susan Powell*, from Cincinnati."

"Well, then, how'd you come to be up at the Pint in the *mornin'* — in a canoe?"

"I warn't up at the Pint in the mornin'."

"It's a lie." The doctor he up and says:

"Would you know the boy again if you was to see him, Hines?"

"I reckon I would, but I don't know. Why, yonder he is, now. I know him perfectly easy."

It was me he pointed at. The doctor says:

"Neighbours, I don't know whether the new couple is frauds or not; but I think it's our duty to see that they don't get away from here till we've looked into this thing. Come along, Hines; come along, the rest of you. We'll take these fellows to the tavern and affront them with t'other couple, and I reckon we'll find out *something* before we get through."

It was about sundown. The doctor he led me along by the hand, and was plenty kind enough, but he never let go my hand.

We all got in a big room in the hotel, and lit up some candles, and fetched in the new couple. First, the doctor says:

"I don't wish to be too hard on these two men, but I think they're frauds, and they may have' complices that we don't know nothing about. If they have, won't the complices get away with that bag of gold Peter Wilks left? It ain't unlikely. If these men ain't frauds, then they won't object to sending for that money and letting us keep it till they prove they're right — ain't that so?"

Everybody agreed to that. So I judged they had our gang in a pretty tight place, right at the outstart. But the king he only looked sorrowful, and says:

"Gentlemen, I wish the money was there, for I ain't go no disposition to throw anything in the way of a fair, open, out-and-out investigation o'this misable business; but alas! the money ain't there; you k'n send and see, if you want to."

"Where is it, then?"

"Well, when my niece give it to me to keep for her, I took and hid it inside o' the straw tick o' my bed, not wishin' to bank it for the few days we'd be here, and considerin' the bed a safe place, we not bein' used to niggers, and suppos'n' 'em honest, like servants in England. The niggers stole it the very next mornin' after I had went downstairs; and when I sold 'em I hadn't missed the money yit, so they got clean away with it. My servant here k'n tell you 'bout it, gentlemen."

The doctor and several said "Shucks!" and I see nobody didn't altogether believe him. One man asked me if I see the niggers steal it. I said. "No" but I see them sneaking out of the room and hustling away, and I never thought nothing, only I reckoned they was afraid they had waked up my master and was trying to get away before he made trouble with them. That was all they asked me. Then the doctor whirls on me and says:

"Are *you* English too?"

I says "Yes" and him and some others laughed, and said "Stuff!"

Well, then they sailed in on the general investigation, and there we had it, up and down, hour in, hour out, and nobody never said a word about supper, nor ever seemed to think about it — and so they kept it up, and kept it up; and it *was* the worst mixed-up thing you ever see. They made the king tell his yarn, and they made the old gentleman tell his'n; and anybody but a lot of prejudiced chuckleheads would a seen that the old gentleman was spinning truth and the other one lies. And by-and-by they had me up to tell what I knowed. The king he give me a left-handed look out of the corner of his eye, and so I knowed enough to talk on the right side. I begun to tell about Sheffield, and how we lived there, and all about the English Wilkses, and so on; but I didn't get pretty fur till the doctor begun to laugh; and Levi Bell, the lawyer, says:

"Set down, my boy, I wouldn't strain myself, if I was you. I reckon you ain't used to lying, it don't seem to come handy; what you want is practice. You do it pretty awkward."

I didn't care nothing for the compliment, but I was glad to be let off, anyway.

The old gentleman broke in, and says:

"I've thought of something. Is there anybody here that helped to lay out my br — helped to lay out the late Peter Wilks for burying?"

"Yes," says somebody, me and Ab Turner done it. We're both here."

Then the old man turns towards the king, and says: "Per'aps this gentleman can tell me what was tattooed on his breast?"

Blamed if the king didn't have to brace up mighty quick, because how was he going to know what was tattooed on the man? He whitened a little; he couldn't help it; and it was mighty still in there, and everybody bending a little forwards and gazing at him. Anyway, he set there, and pretty soon he begun to smile, and says:

"Mf! It's a *very* tough question, *ain't* it? *Yes*, sir, I k'n tell you what's tattooed on his breast. It's jest a small, thin, blue arrow — that's what it is; and if you don't look clost, you can't see it. *Now* what do you say — hey?"

Well, I never see anything like that old blister for clean out-and-out cheek.

The new old gentleman turns brisk towards Ab Turner and his pard, and his eye lights up like he judged he had got the king this time, and says:

"There — you've heard what he said! Was there any such mark on Peter Wilks's breast?"

Both of them spoke up and says:

"We didn't see no such mark."

"Good!" says the old gentleman. "Now, what you *did* see on his breast was a small dim P, and a B (which is an initial he dropped ,when he was young), and a W, with dashes between them, so: P — B — W" — and he marked them that way on a piece of paper.

"Come — ain't that what you saw?"

Both of them spoke up again, and says:

"No, we *didn't*. We never see any marks at all."

Well, everybody was in a state of mind now; and they sings out:

"The whole bilin' of 'm's frauds! Le's duck 'em! le's drown 'em! le's ride 'em on a rail!" and everybody was whooping at once, and there was a rattling pow-wow. But the lawyer he jumps on the table and yells, and says:

"Gentlemen — gentlemen! Hear me just a word — just a single word — if you PLEASE! There's one way yet — let's go and dig up the corpse and look."

That took them.

"We'll do it!" they all shouted: "and if we don't find them marks we'll lynch the whole gang!"

I was scared, now, I tell you. But there warn't no getting away, you know. They gripped us all, and marched us right along, straight for the graveyard, which was a mile and a half down the river, and the whole town at our heels, for we made noise enough, and it was only nine in the evening.

When they got there they swarmed into the graveyard and washed over it like on overflow. And when they got to the grave, they found they had about a hundred times as many shovels as they wanted, but nobody hadn't thought to fetch a lantern. But they sailed into digging, anyway, by the flicker of the lightning, and sent a man to the nearest house a half mile off, to borrow one.

So they dug and dug, like everything; and it got awful dark, and the rain started, and the wind swished and swushed along and the lightning come brisker and brisker, and the thunder boomed.

At last they got out the coffin, and begun to unscrew the lid, and then such another crowding, and shouldering, and shoving as there was, to scrouge in and get a sight, you never see; and in the dark, that way, it was awful.

All of a sudden the lightning let go a perfect sluice of white glare, and somebody sings out:

"By the living jingo, here's the bag of gold on his breast!"

Hines let out a whoop, like everybody else, and dropped my wrist and give a big surge to bust his way in and get a look, and the way I lit out and shinned for the road in the dark, there ain't nobody can tell.

The minute I was far enough above the town to see I could make the tow-head, I begun to look sharp for a boat to borrow; and the first time the lightning showed me one that wasn't chained, I snatched it and shoved. It was a canoe, and warn't fastened with nothing but a rope. The tow-head was a rattling big distance off, away out there in the middle of the river, but I didn't lose no time; and when I struck the raft at last, I was so fagged I would a just laid down to blow and gasp if I could afforded it. But I didn't. As I sprang aboard I sung out:

"Out with you, Jim, and set her loose! Glory be to goodness, we're shut of them!"

Jim lit out, and was a coming for me with both arms spread he was so full of joy; but when I glimpsed him in the lightning, my heart shot up in my mouth, and I went overboard backwards; for I forgot he was old King Lear and a drownded Arab all in one, and it most scared the livers and lights out of me. But Jim fished me out, and was going to hug me and bless me, and so on, he was so glad I was back and we was shut of the king and the duke, but I says:

"Not now — have it for breakfast, have it for breakfast! Cut loose and let her slide!"

So, in two seconds, away we went, a sliding down the river, and it did seem so good to be free again and all by ourselves on the big river and nobody to bother us. I had to skip around a bit, and jump up and crack my heels a few times, I couldnt' help it; but about the third crack I noticed a sound that I knowed mighty well — and held my breath and listened and waited — and sure enough, when the next flash busted out over the water, here they come! — and just a laying to their oars and making their skiff hum! It was the king and the duke.

CHAPTER SIXTEEN

A Royal Row

When they got aboard, the king went for me, and shook me by the collar, and says:

"Tryin' to give us the slip, was ye, you pup! Tired of our company — hey?"

I says:

"Honest, I'll tell you everything, just as it happened, your Majesty. The man that had aholt of me was very good to me, and kept saying he had a boy about as big as me that died last year, and he was sorry to see a boy in such a dangerous fix; and when they was all took by surprise by finding the gold, and made a rush for the coffin, he lets go of me and whispers, 'Heel it, now, or they'll hang ye, sure! 'and I lit out.

"Oh, yes, it's *mighty* likely!" and he shook me up again and said he reckoned he'd drownd me. But the duke says:

"Leggo the boy, you old idiot! Would you a done any different? Did you inquire around for him, when you got loose? I don't remember it."

So the king let go of me, and begun to cuss that town and everybody in it. But the duke says:

"You better a blame sight give yourself a good cussing, for you're the one that's entitled to it most. You hain't done a thing, from the start, that had any sense in it, except coming out so cool and cheeky with that imaginary blue-arrow mark. But that trick took 'em to the graveyard, and the gold done us a still bigger kindness; for if the excited fools hadn't let go all holts and made that rush to get a look, we'd a slept in our cravats tonight — cravats warranted to *wear*, too — longer than *we'd* need 'em."

They was still a minute — thinking — then the king says, kind of absent-minded like:

"Mf! and we reckoned the *niggers* stole it!"

That made me squirm!

"Yes," says the duke, kinder slow, and deliberate, and sarcastic, "*we* did."

The king kind of ruffles up, and says:

"Looky here, Bilgewater, what'r your referrin' to?"

The duke bristles right up now, and says:

"Oh, let up on this cussed nonsense — do you take me for a blame' fool? Don't you reckon I know who hid that money in that coffin?"

"*Yes,* sir! I know you do know — because you done it yourself!"

"It's a lie!" — and the duke went for him. The king sings out: "Take y'r hands off! — leggo my throat! — I take it all back!"

The duke says:

"Well, you just own up, first, that you did hide that money there, intending to give me the slip one of these days, and come back and dig it up, and have it all to yourself."

The king begun to gurgle, and then he gasps out:

" 'Nough! — I *own up!*"

I was very glad to hear him say that, it made me feel much more easier than what I was feeling before. So the duke took his hands off, and says:

"If you ever deny it again, I'll drown you. Cuss you, I can see, now, why you was so anxious to make up the deffesit — you wanted to get what money I'd got out of the Nonesuch, and one thing or another, and scoop it *all!*"

The king says, timid, and still a snuffling:

"Why, Duke, it was you that said make up the deffesit, it warn't me."

"Dry up! I don't want to hear no more out of you!" says the duke. "And *now* you see what you got by it. They've got all their own money back, and all of ourn but a shekel or two, *besides.* G'long to bed — and don't you deffesit me no more deffesits, long's you live!"

So the king sneaked into the wigwam, and took to his bottle for comfort; and before long the duke tackled *his* bottle; and so in about half an hour they was as thick as thieves again, and the tighter they got, the lovinger they got; and went off a snoring in each other's arms. Of course when they got to snoring, we had a long gabble, and I told Jim everything.

We dasn't stop again at any town, for days and days; kept right along down the river. We was down south in the warm weather, now, and a mighty long ways from home. So now the frauds reckoned they was out of danger, and they begun to work the villages again.

Well, early one morning we hid the raft in a good safe place about two mile below a little bit of a shabby village, named Pikesville, and the king he went ashore, and told us all to stay hid whilst he went up to town and smelt around to see if anybody had got any wind of the Royal Nonesuch there yet.

So we stayed where we was. The duke he fretted and sweated around, and was in a mighty sour way. I was good and glad when midday come and no king; we could have a change, anyway — and maybe a chance for the change, on top of it. So me and the duke went up to the village, and hunted around there for the king, and by-and-by we found him in the back room of a little low doggery very tight, and a lot of loafers bullyragging him for sport, and he a cussing and threatening with all his might, and so tight he couldn't walk, and couldn't do nothing to them. The duke he begun to abuse him for an old fool, and the king begun to sass back; and the minute they was fairly at it, I lit out, and shook the reefs out of my hind legs, and spun down the river road like a deer — for I see our chance; and I made up my mind that it would be a long day before they ever see me and Jim again. I got down there all out of breath but loaded up with joy, and sung out.

"Set her loose, Jim, we're all right, now!"

But there warn't no answer, and nobody come out of the wigwam. Jim was gone! I set up a shout — and then another — and then another one; and run this way and that in the woods whooping and screeching; but it warn't no use — old Jim was gone. Then I set down and cried; I couldn't help it. But I couldn't set still long. Pretty soon I went out on the road, trying to think what I better do, and I run across a boy walking, and asked him if he'd seen a strange nigger, dressed so and so, and he says:

"Yes."

"Whereabouts?" says I.

"Down to Silas Phelps' place, two mile below here. He's a runaway nigger, and they've got him."

"It's a good job they got him."

"Well, I reckon! There's two hundred dollars reward on him."

"Who nailed him?"

"It was an old fellow — a stranger — and he sold out his chance in him for forty dollars, becuz he's got to go up the river and can't wait."

"Maybe there's something ain't straight about it."

"But it is, though — straight as a string. Say, gimme a chaw tobacker, won't ye?"

I didn't have none, so he left. I went to the raft, and set down in the wigwam to think. But I couldn't come to nothing. I thought till I wore my head sore, but I couldn't see no way out of the trouble. After all this long journey, and after all we'd done for them scoundrels, here was it all come to nothing, everything all busted up and ruined, because they could have the heart to serve Jim such a trick as that, and make him a slave again all his life, and amongst strangers, too, for forty dirty dollars.

Straightaway I knew I'd have to try to steal him free again.

So then I took the bearings of a woody island that was down the river a piece, and as soon as it was fairly dark I crept out with my raft and went for it, and hid it there, and then turned in. I slept the night through, and got up before it was light, and had my breakfast, and put on my store clothes, and tied up some others and one thing or another in a bundle, and took the canoe and cleared for shore. I landed below where I judged was Phelps' place, and hid my bundle in the woods, and then filled up the canoe with water, and loaded rocks into her and sunk her where I could find her again when I wanted her, about a quarter of a mile below a little steam sawmill that was on the bank.

Then I struck up the road, and when I passed the mill I see a sign on it, "Phelps' Sawmill", and when I come to the farmhouses, two or three hundred yards further along, I kept my eyes peeled, but didn't see nobody around, though it was good daylight, now.

Phelps' was one of these little one-horse cotton plantations; and they all look alike.

I went around and clumb over the back stile by the ash-hopper, and started for the kitchen. I went right along, not fixing up any particular plan, but just trusting to Providence to put the right words in my mouth if I left it alone.

When I got half-way, first one hound and then another got up and went for me, and of course I stopped and faced them and kept still. And such another pow-wow as they made! In a quarter of a minute I was a kind of a hub of a wheel, as you may say — spokes made out of dogs — circle of fifteen of them packed together around me, with their necks and noses stretched up towards me, a barking and howling.

A nigger woman came tearing out of the kitchen with a rolling-pin in her hand, singing out, "Begone! you Tige! you Spot! begone, sah!"

And behind the woman comes a little nigger girl and two little nigger boys, without anything on but two-linen shirts, and they hung on to their mother's gown, and peeped out from behind her at me, bashful, the way they always do. And here comes the white woman running from the house, about forty-five or fifty years ald, bare-headed, and her spinning-stick in her hand; and behind her comes her little white children, acting the same way the little niggers was doing. She was smiling all over so she could hardly stand — and says:

"It's you, at last! — ain't it?"

I out with a "Yes'm", before I thought.

She grabbed me and hugged me tight; and then gripped me by both hands and shook and shook; and the tears come in her eyes, and run down over; and she couldn't seem to hug and shake enough and kept saying, "You don't look as much like your mother as I reckoned you would, but law sakes, I don't care for that, I'm so glad to see you! Dear, dear, it does seem like I could eat you up! Children, it's your Cousin Tom! — tell him howdy."

But they ducked their heads, and put their fingers in their mouths and hid behind her. So she run on:

"Lize, hurry up and get him a hot breakfast, right away — or did you get your breakfast on the boat?"

I said I had got it on the boat. So then she started for the house, leading me by the hand, and the children tagging after. When we got there, she set me down in a split-bottomed chair, and set herself down on a low stool in front of me, and says:

"How'd you get your breakfast so early on the boat?"

It was kinder thin ice, but I says:

"The captain see me standing around, and told me I better have something to eat before I went ashore; so he took me in the texas to the officers' lunch, and give me all I wanted."

I was getting so uneasy I couldn't think good. I had my mind on the children all the time; I wanted to get them out to one side and pump them a little, and find out who I was. Pretty soon she made the cold chills streak all down my back, because she says:

"But here we're a running on this way, and you hain't told me a word about Sis, nor any of them. Now I'll rest my works a little, and you start up yourn; just tell me everything — tell me all about'm all — every one of 'm; and how they are, and what they're doing, and what they told you to tell me; and every last thing you can think of."

Well, I see I was up a stump — and up it good. Providence had stood by me this fur, all right, but I was hard and tight aground, now. I see it warn't a bit of use to try to go ahead — I'd got to throw up my hand. So I says to myself, here's another place where I got to risk the truth. I opened my mouth to begin; but she grabbed me and hustled me in behind the bed, and says:

"Here he comes! stick your head down lower — there that'll do; you can't be seen now. Don't you let on you're here. I'll play a joke on him. Children, don't you say a word."

I had just one little glimpse of the old gentleman when he comes in, then the bed hid him. Mrs. Phelps she jumps for him and says: "Has he come?"

"No," says her husband.

"Good-ness gracious!" she says, "what in the world can have become of him?"

"I can't imagine", says the old gentleman; "and I must say, it makes me dreadful uneasy."

"Why, Silas! Look younder! Up the road! — ain't that somebody coming?"

He sprung to the window at the head of the bed, and that give Mrs. Phelps the chance she wanted. She stooped down quick, at the foot of the bed, and give me a pull, and out I come; and when he turned back from the window, there she stood, a-beaming and a-smiling like a house afire, and I standing pretty meek and sweaty alongside. The old gentleman stared, and says:

"Why, who's that?"

"Who do you reckon't is?"

"I hain't no idea. Who is it?"

"It's Tom Sawyer!"

By jinks, I most slumped through the floor. But there warn't no time to swap knives; the old man grabbed me by the hand and shook, and kept on shaking; and all the time, how the woman did dance around and laugh and cry; and then how they both did fire off questions about Sid, and Mary, and the rest of the tribe.

But if they was joyful, it warn't nothing to what I was; for it was like being born again, I was so glad to find out who I was. Well, they froze to me for two hours; and at last when my chin was so tired it couldn't hardly go, any more, I had told them more about my family — I mean the Sawyer family — than ever happened to any six Sawyer families.

Being Tom Sawyer was easy and comfortable; and it stayed easy and comfortable till by-and-by I hear a steamboat coughing along down the river — then I says to myself, s'pose Tome Sawyer come down on that boat? and s'pose he steps in here, any minute, and sings out my name before I can throw him a wink to keep quiet? Well, I couldn't have it that way — it wouldn't do at all. So I told the folks I reckoned I would go up to the town and fetch down my baggage. The old gentleman was for going along with me, but I said no, I could drive the horse myself, and I druther he wouldn't take no trouble about me.

CHAPTER SEVENTEEN

Southern Hospitality

So I started for town, in the wagon, and when I was half-way I see a wagon coming, and sure enough it was Tom Sawyer, and I stopped and waited till he come along. I says, "Hold on!" and it stopped alongside, and his mouth opened like a trunk, and stayed so; and he swallowed two or three times like a person that's got a dry throat, and then says:

"I hain't ever done you no harm. You know that. So, then, what you want to come back and ha'nt me for?"

I says:

"I hain't come back — I hain't been gone."

When he heard my voice, it righted him up some, but he warn't quite satisfied yet. He says:

"Don't you play nothing on me, because I wouldn't on you. Honest injun, now, you ain't a ghost?"

"Honest injun, I ain't" I says.

And he wanted to know all about it right off; because it was a grand adventure, and mysterious, and so it hit him where he lived. But I said, leave it alone till by-and-by; and told his driver to wait, and we drove off a little piece, and I told him the kind of a fix I was in, and what did he reckon we better do?

"It's all right, I've got it. Take my trunk in your wagon, and let on it's your'n; and you turn back and fool along slow, so as to get to the house about the time you ought to; and I'll go towards town a piece, and take a fresh start, and get there a quarter or half an hour after you; and you needn't let on to know me, at first."

I says:

"All right; but wait a minute. There's one more thing — a thing that nobody don't know but me. And that is, there's a nigger here that I'm a trying to steal out of slavery — and his name is Jim — old Miss Watson's Jim."

His eye lit up, and he says:

"I'll help you steal him!"

"Oh, shucks," I says, "you're joking."

"I ain't joking, either."

"Well, then," I says, "joking or no joking, if you hear anything said about a runaway nigger, don't forget to remember that you don't know nothing about him, and I don't know nothing about him."

Then we took the trunk and put it in my wagon, and he drove off his way, and I drove mine.

In about half an hour Tom's wagon drove up to the front stile, and Aunt Sally she see it through the window because it was only about fifty yards, and says:

"Why, there's somebody come! I wonder who'tis? Why, I do believe it's a stranger. Jimmy," (that's one of the children,) "run and tell Lize to put on another plate for dinner."

Tom had his store clothes on, and an audience — and that was always nuts for Tom Sawyer. When he got afront of us, he lifts his hat ever so gracious and dainty, like it was the lid of a box that had butterflies asleep in it, and he didn't want to disturb them, and says:

"Mr. Archibald Nichols, I presume?"

"No, my boy," says the old gentleman, "I'm sorry to say't your driver had deceived you; Nichols's place is down a matter of three mile more. Come in, come in."

So Tom he thanked them very hearty and handsome, and let himself be persuaded, and come in; and when he was in, he said he was a stranger from Hicksville, Ohio and his name was William Thompson — and he made another bow.

Well, he run on, and on, and on, making up stuff about Hicksville and everybody in it he could invent, and I getting a little nervous, and wondering how this was going to help me out of my scrape; and at last, still talking along, he reached over and kissed Aunt Sally right on the mouth, and then settled back in his chair, comfortable, and was going on talking; but she jumped up and wiped it off with the back of her hand, and says:

"You owdacious puppy!"

He looked kind of hurt, and says:

"I'm surprised at you, m'am."

"You're s'rp — Why, what do you reckon I am? I've a good notion to tale and — say, what do you mean by kissing me?"

Then he looks on around, to me — and says:

"Tom, didn't you think Aunty Sally'd open out her arms and say, 'Sid Sawyer —'"

"My land!" she says, breaking in and jumping for him, "you impudent young rascal, to fool a body so —"

So she didn't lose no time, but hugged him and kissed him, over and over again, and then turned him over to the old man, and he took what was left. And after they got a little quiet again, she says:

"Why, dear me, I never see such a surprise. We warn't looking for you, at all, but only Tom. Sid never wrote to me about anybody coming but him."

"It's because it warn't intended for any of us to come but Tom," he says: "but I begged and begged, and at the last minute she let me come, too; so, coming down the river, me and Tom thought it would be a first-rate surprise for him to come here to the house first, and for me to by-and-by tag along and drop in and let on to be a stranger."

There was a considerable good deal of talk, all the afternoon, and me and Tom was on the look-out all the time, but it warn't no use, they didn't happen to say nothing about any runaway nigger, and we was afraid to try to work up to it. But at supper, at night, one of the little boys, says:

"Pa, mayn't Tom and Sid and me go to the show?"

"No," says the old man, "I reckon there ain't going to be any; and you couldn't go if there was; because the runaway nigger told Burton and me all about that scandalous show, and Burton said he could tell the people; so I reckon they've drove the owdacious loafers out of town before this time."

So there it was! But I couldn't help it. Tom and me was to sleep in the same room and bed; so, being tired, we bid goodnight and went up to bed, right after supper, and clumb out of the window and down the lightning-rod, and shoved for the town; for I didn't believe anybody was going to give the king and the duke a hint, and so, if I didn't hurry up and give them one they'd get into trouble sure.

I told Tom all about our Royal Nonesuch rapscallions, and as much of the raft-voyage as I had time to; and as we struck into the town and up through the middle of it — it was as much as half after height, then — here comes a raging rush of people, with torches, and an awful whooping and yelling, and banging tin pans and blowing horns; and we jumped to one side to let them go by; and as they went by, I see they had the king and the duke astraddle of a rail — that is, I knowed it was the king and the duke, though they was all over tar and feathers, and didn't look like nothing in the world that was human — just looked like a couple of monstrous big soldier-plumes. Well, it made me sick to see it; and I was sorry for them poor pitiful rascals, it seemed like I couldn't ever feel any hardness against them any more in the world. It was a dreadful thing to see. Human beings can be awful cruel to one another.

By-and-by Tom says:

"Looky here, Huck, what fools we are, to not think of it before! I bet I know where Jim is."

"No! Where?"

"In that hut down by the ash-hopper. Why, looky here. When we was at dinner, didn't you see a nigger man go in there with some vittles?"

"Yes."

"What did you think the vittles was for?"

"For a dog."

"So'd I. Well, it wasn't for a dog."

"Why?"

"Because part of it was water-melon."

"So it was — I noticed it. Well, it does beat all, that I never thought about a dog not eating water-melon. It shows how a body can see and don't see at the same time."

"Well, the nigger unlocked the padlock when he went in, and he locked it again when he come out. He fetched uncle a key, about the time we got up from table, same key, I bet. Water-melon shows man, lock shows prisoner; and it ain't likely there's two prisoners on such a little plantation, and where the people's all so kind and good. Jim's the prisoner. All right — I'm glad we found it out detective fashion. I wouldn't give shucks for any other way."

When we got home, the house was all dark and still; so we went on down to the hut by the ash-hopper, for to examine it. We went through the yard, so as to see what the hounds would do. They knowed us, and didn't make no more noise than country dogs in always doing when anything comes by in the night. When we got to the cabin, we took a look at the front and the two sides; and on the side I warn't acquainted with — which was the north side

— we found a square window-hole, up tolerable high, with just one stout board nailed across it. I says:

"Here's the ticket. This hole's big enough for Jim to get through, if we wrench off the board."

Tom says:

"It's as simple as tit-tat-toe, three-in-a-row, and as easy as playing hooky. I should hope we can find a way that's a little more complicated than that, Huck Finn."

"Well, then," I says, "how'll it do to saw him out, the way I done before I was murdered, that time?"

"That's more like,", he says. "It's real mysterious, and troublesome, and good," he says; "but I bet we can find a way that's twice as long. There ain't no hurry, let's keep on looking around."

Betwixt the hut and the fence, on the back side, was a lean-to, that joined the hut at the eaves, and was made out of plank. It was as long as the hut, but narrow — only about six feet wide. The door to it was at the south end, and was padlocked. Tom he went to the soap kettle, and searched around and fetched back the iron thing they lift the lid with; so he took it and prized out one of the staples. The chain fell down, and we opened the door and went in, and shut it, and struck a match, and see the shed was only built against the cabin and hadn't no connexion with it; and there warn't no floor to the shed, nor nothing in it but some old rusty played-out hoes, and spades, and picks, and a crippled plough. The match went out, and so did we, and shoved in the staple again, and the door was locked as good as ever. Tom was joyful. He says: "Now we're all right. We'll dig him out. It'll take about a week!"

In the morning we was up at break of day, and down to the nigger cabins to pet the dogs and make friends with the nigger that fed Jim — if it was Jim that was being fed.

The niggers was just getting through breakfast and starting for the fields; and Jim's nigger was piling up a tin pan with bread and meat and things; and whilst the others was leaving, the key come from the house.

So Tom says:

"What's the vittles for? Going to feed the dogs?"

The nigger kind of smiled around gradually over his face, like when you heave a brickbat in a mud puddle, and he says:

"Yes, Mars Sid, a dog. Cur'us dog, too. Does you want to go en look at'im?"

"Yes."

I hunched Tom, and whispers:

"You going, right here in the day-break? That warn't the plan."

"No, it warn't — but it's the plan now."

So, drat him, we went along, but I didn't like it much When we got in, we couldn't hardly see anything, it was so dark. But Jim was there, sure enough.

Tom says:

"I wonder if Uncle Silas is going to hang this nigger. If I was to catch a nigger that was ungrateful enough to run away, I wouldn't give him up, I'd hang him." And whilst the nigger stepped to the door, he whispers to Jim, and says:

"Don't ever let on to know us. And if you hear any digging going on night, it's us; we're going to set you free."

Jim only had time to grab us by the hand and squeeze it, then the nigger come back, and we said we'd come again some time if the nigger wanted us to; and he said he would, more particular if it was dark, because it was good to have folks around then.

CHAPTER EIGHTEEN

The Plot Thickens

As soon as we reckoned everybody was asleep, that night, we went down the lightning-rod, and shut ourselves up in the lean-to, and went to work. We cleared everything out of the way, about four or five feet along the middle of the bottom log. Tom said he was right behind Jim's bed now, and we'd dig in under it, and when we got through there couldn't nobody in the cabin ever know there was any hole there, because Jim's counterpin hung down most to the ground, and you'd have to raise it up and look under to see the hole. So we dug and dug, with case-knives, till most midnight; and then we was dog-tired, and our hands was blistered, and yet you couldn't see we'd done anything hardly. At last I says:

"Well, what are we going to do, Tom?"

I'll tell you. It ain't right, and it ain't moral, and I wouldn't like it to get out — but there ain't only just the one way; we got to dig him out with the picks, and let on it's case-knives."

"Now you're talking!" I says: "your head gets leveller and leveller all the time, Tom Sawyer," I says. "Picks is the thing, moral or no moral; and as for me, I don't care shucks for the morality of it, nohow. When I start in to steal a nigger, or a water-melon, or a Sunday-school book, I ain't no ways particular how it's done so it's done. What I want is my nigger; or what I want is my water-melon; or what I want is my Sunday-school book; and if a pick's the handiest thing, that's the thing I'm a-going to dig that nigger, or that water-melon or that Sunday-school book out with; and I don't give a dead rat what the authorities thinks about it nuther."

So then I got a shovel, and then we picked and shovelled, turn about, and made the fur fly. We stuck to it about half an hour, which was as long as we could stand up; but we had a good deal of a hole to show for it.

That next night we went down the lightning-rod a little after ten, and took one of the candles along, and listened under the window-hole, and heard Jim snoring; so we pitched it in, and it didn't wake him. Then we whirled in with the pick and shovel, and in about two hours and a half the job was done. We crept in under Jim's bed and into the cabin, and pawed around and found the candle and lit it, and stood over Jim a while, and found him looking hearty and healthy, and then we woke him up gentle and gradual. He was so glad to see us he most cried; and called us honey, and all the pet names he could think of; and was for having us hunt up a cold chisel to cut the chain off of his leg with, right away, and clearing out without losing any time. But Tom he showed him how unregular it would be, and set down and told him all about our plans, and how he could alter them in a minute any time there was an alarm; and not to be the least afraid, because we would see he got away, sure. So Jim he said it was all right, and we set there and talked over old times a while, and then Tom asked a lot of questions, and when Jim told him Uncle Silas come in every day or two to pray with him, and Aunt Sally come in to see if he was comfortable and had plenty to eat, and both of them was kind as they could be.

Jim had plenty corn-cob pipes, and tobacco; so we had a right down good sociable time; then we crawled out through the hole, and so, home to bed, with hands that looked like they'd been chawed. Tom was in high spirits. He said it was the best fun he ever had in his life, and the most intellectual; and said if he only could see his way to it we would keep it up all the rest of our lives and leave Jim to our children to get out; for he believed Jim would come to like it better and better the more he got used to it. He said that in that way it could be strung out to as much as eighty years, and would be the best time on record. And he said it would make us all celebrated that had a hand in it.

In the morning we went up to the wood-pile and chopped up the brass candlestick into handy sizes, and Tom put them and a pewter spoon in his pocket. Then we went to the nigger cabins, and while I got Nat's notice off, Tom shoved a piece of candlestick into the middle of a corn-pone that was in Jim's pan, and we went along with Nat to see how it would work, and it just worked noble; when Jim bit into it, it most mashed all his teeth out; and there warn't ever anything could a worked better. Tom said so himself. Jim he never let on but what it was only just a piece of rock or something like that that's always getting into bread, you know; but after that he never bit into nothing but what he jabbed his fork into it in three or four places, first.

And whilst we was a standing there in the dimmish light, here comes a couple of the hounds bulging in, from under Jim's bed; and they kept on piling in till there was eleven of them, and there warn't hardly room in there to get your breath. By jings, we forgot to fasten the lean-to door. The nigger Nat he only just hollered ,,Witches!" once, and keeled over onto the floor amongst the dogs, and begun to groan like he was dying. Tom jerked the door open and flung out a slab of Jim's meat, and the dogs went for it, and in two seconds he was out himself and back again and shut the door, and I knowed he'd fixed the other door too. Then he went to work on the nigger, coaxing him and petting him, and asking him if he'd been imagining he saw something again. He raised up, and blinked his eyes around, and says:

"Mars Sid, you'll say I's a fool, but if I didn't b'lieve I see most a million dogs, er devils, er some'n, I wisht I may die

138

right heah in dese tracks. I did, mos' sholy. Mars Sid, I felt um — I felt um, sah; dey was all over me. Dad fetch it, I jis' wisht I could git my han's on one er dem witches jis' wunst — on'y jis' wunst — it's all I'd ast. But mos'ly I wisht dey'd lemme 'lone, I does."

Tom says:

"Well, I tell you what I think. What makes them come here just at this runaway nigger's breakfast-time? It's because they're hungry; that's the reason. You make them a witch pie; that's the thing for you to do."

"But, my lan', Mars Sid, how's I gwyne to make'm a witch pie? I doan'know how to make it. I hain't ever hearn er sich a thing b'fo'."

"Well, then, I'll have to make it myself."

"Will you do it, honey? Will you? I'll wusshup de groun' und'yo'foot, I will!"

"All right, I'll do it, seeing it's you, and you'e been good to us and showed us the runaway nigger. But you got to be mighty careful. When we come around, your turn your back and then whatever we've put in the pan, don't you let on you see it at all. And don't you look, when Jim unloads the pan — something might happen, I don't know what. And above all, don't you *handle* the witch-things."

"*Hannel'm*, Mars Sid? What is you a talkin'bout? I wouldn't lay de weight er my finger on um, not f'r ten hund'd thous'n' billion dollars, I wouldn't."

That was all fixed. So then we went away and went to the rubbage-pile in the back yard where they keep the old boots, and rags, and pieces of bottles, and wore-out tin things, and all such truck, and scratched around and found an old tin washpan and stopped up the holes as well as we could, to bake the pie in, and took it down cellar and stole it full of flour, and started for breakfast and found a couple of shin-gle-nails that Tom said would be handy for a prisoner to scrabble his name and sorrows on the dungeon wall with, and dropped one of them in Aunt Sally's apron pocket which was hanging on a chair, and t'other we stuck in the band of Uncle Silas's hat, which was on the bureau, because we heard the children say their pa and ma was going to the runaway nigger's house this morning, and then went to breakfast, and Tom dropped the pewter spoon in Uncle Silas's coat pocket, and Aunt Sally wasn't come yet, so we had to wait a little while.

And when she come she was hot, and red, and cross, and couldn't hardly wait for the blessing; and then she went to sluicing out coffee with one hand and cracking the handiest child's head with her thimble with the other, and says:

"I've hunted high, and I've hunted low, and it does beat all, what has become of your other shirt."

My heart fell down amongst my lungs and livers and things, and a hard piece of corn-crust started down my throat after it and got met on the road with a cough and was shot across the table and took one of the children in the eye and curled him up like a fishing-worm, and let a cry out of him the size of a war-whoop, and Tom he turned kinder blue around the gills, and it all amounted to a considerable state of things for about a quarter of a minute or as much at that, and I would a sold out for half price if there was a bidder. But after that we was all right again — it was the sudden surprise of it that knocked us so kind of cold. Uncle Silas he says:

"It's most uncommon curious, I can't understand it. I know perfectly well I took if off, because." —

"Because you hain't got but one on. Just listen at the man! I know you took it off, and know it by a better way than your wool-gathering memory, too, because it was on the clo'es-line yesterday — I see it there myself. But it's gone — that's the long and the short of it, and you'll just

have to change to a red flann'l one till I can get time to make
a new one. And it'll be the third I've made in two years; it
just keeps a body on the jump to keep you in shirts; and
whatever you do manage to do with'm all, is more'n I can
make out. A body'd think you would learn to take some sort
of care of'em, at your time of life."

"I know it, Sally, and I do try all I can. But it oughtn't
to be altogether my fault, because you know I don't see them
nor have nothing to do with them except when they're on
me; and I don't believe I've ever lost one of them off of me."

"Well, it ain't your fault if you haven't, Silas — you'd a
done it if you could, I reckon. And the shirt ain't all that's
gone, nuther. Ther's a spoon gone; and that ain't all. There was
ten, and now ther's only nine. The calf got the shirt I reckon,
but the calf never took the spoon, that's certain."

"Why, what else is gone, Sally?"

"Ther's six candles gone — that's what. The rats could a
got the candles, and I reckon they did; I wonder they don't
walk off with the whole place, the way you're always going
to stop their holes and don't do it; and if they warn't
fools they'd sleep in your hair, Silas — you'd never find it
out; but you can't lay the spoon on the rats, and that I know."

"Well, Sally, I'm in fault, and I acknowledge it; I've been
remiss; but I won't let tomorrow go by without stopping up
them holes."

"Oh, I wouldn't hurry, next year'll do. Matilda Angelina
Araminta Phelps!"

Whack comes the thimble, and the child snatches her claws
out of the sugar-bowl without fooling around any. Just then,
the nigger woman steps onto the passage, and says:

"Missus, dey's a sheet gone."

"A sheet gone! Well, for the land's sake!"

"I'll stop them holes today", says Uncle Silas, looking sorrowful.

"Oh, do shet up! — S'pose the rats took the sheet? Where's it gone, Lize?"

"Clah to goodness I hain't no notion, Miss Sally. She wuz on de clo's-line yistiddy, but she done gone; she ain' dah no mo', now."

"I reckon the world is coming to an end. I never see the beat of it, in all my born days. A shirt, and a sheet, and a spoon, and six can —"

"Missus," comes a young yaller wench, "dey's a brass cannelstick miss'n."

"Cler out from here, you hussy, er I'll take a skillet to ye!"

Well she was just a biling. I begun to lay for a chance; I reckoned I would sneak out and go for the woods till the weather moderated. She kept a raging right along, running her insurrection all by herself, and everybody else mighty meek and quiet; and at last Uncle Silas, looking kind of foolish, fishes up that spoon out of his pocket. She stopped, with her mouth open and her hands up; and as for me, I wished I was in Jerusalem of somewheres. But not long; because she says:

"It's just as I expected. So you had it in your pocket all the time; and like as not you've got the other things there, too. How'd it get there?"

"I reely don't know, Sally," he says, kind of apologising, "or you know I would tell. I was a-studying over my text in Acts Seventeen, before breakfast, and I reckon I put it in there, not noticing, meaning to put my Testament in, and it must be so, because my Testament ain't in, but I'll go and see, and if the Testament is where I had it, I'll know I didn't put it in, and that will show that I laid the Testament down and took up the spoon, and —"

"Oh, for the land's sake! Give a body a rest! Go 'long now, the whole kit and biling of ye; and don't come nigh me again till I've got back my peace of mind."

I'd a heard her, if she'd a said it to herself, let alone speaking it out; and I'd a got up and obeyed her, if I'd a been dead. As we was passing through the setting-room, the old man he took up his hat, and the shingle-nail fell out on the floor, and he just merely picked it up and laid it on the mantel-shelf, and never said nothing, and went out. Tom see him do it, and remembered about the spoon, and says:

"Well, it ain't no use to send things by him no more, he ain't reliable." Then he says: "But he done us a good turn with the spoon anyway, without knowing it, and so we'll go and do him one without him knowing it — stop up his rat-holes."

There was a noble good lot of them, down cellar, and it took us a whole hour, but we done the job tight and good, and ship-shape. Then we heard steps on the stairs, and blowed out our light, and hid; and here comes the old man, with a candle in one hand and a bundle of stuff in t'other, looking as absent-minded as year before last. He went a mooning around, first to one rat-hole and then to another, till he'd been to them all. Then he stood about five minutes, picking tallow-drip off of his candle and thinking. Then he turns off slow and dreamy towards the stairs, saying:

"Well, for the life of me I can't remember when I done it. I could show her now that I warnt' to blame on account of the rats. But never mind — let it go. I reckon it wouldn't do no good."

And so he went on a mumbling uptairs, and then we left. He was a mighty nice old man. And always is.

Tom was a good deal bothered about what to do for a spoon, but he said we'd got to have it; so he took a think. When he had ciphered it out, he told me how we was to do;

then we went and waited around the spoon-basket till we see Aunt Sally coming, and then Tom went to counting the spoons and laying them out to one side, and I slid one of them up my sleeve, and Tom says:

"Why, Aunt Sally, there ain't but nine spoons, yet."

She says:

"Go 'long to your play, and don't bother me. I know better, I counted them myself."

"Well, I've counted them twice, Aunty, and I can't make but nine."

She looked out of all patience, but of course she come to count — anybody would.

"I declare to gracious ther' ain't but nine!" she says. "Why, what in the world — plague take the things, I'll count m'again."

So I slipped back the one I had, and when she got done counting, she says:

"Hang the troublesome rubbage, ther's ten, now!" and she looked huffy and bothered both. But Tom says:

"Why, Aunty, I don't think there's ten."

"You numskull, didn't you see me count 'm?"

"I know, but —"

"Well, I'll count 'm again."

So I smouched one, and they come out nine same as the other time. Well, she was in a tearing way — just a trembling all over, she was so mad. But she counted and counted, till she got that addled she'd start to count in the basket for a spoon, sometimes, and so, three times they come out right, and three times they come out wrong. Then she grabbed up the basket and slammed it across the house and knocked the cat galley-west; and she said cle'r out and let her have some peace, and if we come bothering around her again betwixt that and dinner, she'd skin us. So we had the odd spoon; and dropped it in her apron pocket whilst she was a giving us our sailing-orders, and Jim got it all right, along with her shingle-nail, before noon. We was very well satisfied with this business, and Tom allowed it was worth twice the trouble it took, because he said now she couldn't ever count them spoons twice alike again to save her life; and wouldn't believe she'd counted them right, if she did: and said that after she'd about counted her head off, for the next three days, he judged she'd give it up and offer to kill anybody that wanted her to ever count them any more.

So we put the sheet back on the line, that night, and stole one out of her closet; and kept on putting it back and stealing it again, for a couple of days, till she didn't know how many sheets she had, any more, and said she didn't care, and warn't agoing to bullyrag the rest of her soul out about it, and wouldn't count them again not to save her life, she druther die first.

So we was all right now, as to the shirt and the sheet and the spoon and the candles, by the help of the calf and the rats and the mixed-up counting; and as to the candlestick, it warn't no consequence, it would blow over by-and-by.

But that pie was a job; we had no end of trouble with that pie. We fixed it up away down in the woods, and cooked it there; and we got it done at last, and very satisfactory, too; but not all in one day; we had to use up three washpans full of flour, before we got through, and we got burnt pretty much all over, in places, and eyes put out with the smoke; because, you see, we didn't want nothing but a crust, and we couldn't prop it up right, and she would always cave in. But, of course, we thought of the right way at last; which was to cook the ladder too, in the pie. So then we laid in with Jim, the second night, and tore up the sheet all in little strings, and twisted them together, and long before daylight we had a lovely rope, that you could a hung a person with. We let on it took nine months to make it.

And in the forenoon we took it down to the woods, but it wouldn't go in the pie. Being made of a whole sheet, that way, there was rope enough for forty pies, if we'd wanted them, and plenty left over for soup, or sausage, of anything you choose. We could a had a whole dinner.

But we didn't need it. All we needed was just enough for the pie, and so we throwed the rest away. We didn't cook none of the pies in the wash-pan, afraid the solder would melt; but Uncle Silas he had a noble brass warming-pan which he thought considerable of, because it belonged to one of his ancestors with a long wooden handle that come over from England with William the Conqueror in the *Mayflower* or one of them early ships and was hid away up garret with a lot of other old pot and things that was valuable, not on account of being any account because they warn't, but on account of them being relicts, you know, and we snaked her out, private, and took her down there, but she failed on the first pies, because we didn't know how, but she come up smiling on the last one. We took and lined her with dough, and set her in the coals, and loaded her up with rag-rope and put on a dough roof, and shut down the lid, and put hot embers on top, and stood off five feet, with the long handle, cool and comfortable; in fifteen minutes she turned out a pie that was a satisfaction to look at. But the person that et it would want to fetch a couple of kags of toothpicks along, for if that rope ladder wouldn't cramp him down to business, I don't know nothing what I'm talking about, and lay him in enough stomach-ache to last him till next time, too.

Nat didn't look, when we put the witch pie in Jim's pan and we put the three tin places in the bottom of the pan under the vittles; and so Jim got everything all right, and as soon as he was by himself he busted into the pie and hid the rope-ladder inside of his straw tick, and scratched some marks on a tin place and throwed it out of the window-hole.

CHAPTER NINETEEN

Unpleasant Glory

Making them pens was a distressid-tough job, and so was the saw; and Jim allowed the inscription was going to be the toughest of all. That's the one which the prisoner has to scrabble on the wall. But we had to have it; Tom said we'd got to: there warn't no case of a state prisoner not scrabbling his inscription to leave behind, and his coat of arms. "Look at Lady Jane Grey," he says: "look at Gilford Dudley; look at old Northumberland! Why, Huck, s'pose it is considerable trouble" — what you going to do? — how you going to get around it? Jim's got to do his inscription and coat of arms. They all do."

Jim says: "Why, Mars Tom, I hain't got no coat o' arms; I hain't got nuffn but dish-yer ole shirt, en you knows I got to keep de journal on dat."

"Oh, you don't understand, Jim; a coat of arms is very different."

"Well,", I says, "Jim's right, anyway, when he says he hain't got no coat of arms, because he hain't."

"I reckon I knowed that,", Tom says, "but you bet he'll have one before he goes out of this — because he's going out right, and there ain't going to be no flaws in his record."

So whilst me and Jim filed away at the pens on a brickbat apiece, Jim a making his'n out of the brass and I making mine out of the spoon, Tom set to work to think out the coat of arms. By-and-by he said he'd struck so many good ones he didn't hardly know which to take, but there was one which he reckoned he'd decide on. He says:

"On the scutcheon we'll have a bend or in the dexter base, a saltire *murrey* in the fess, with a dog, couchant, for common charge, and under his foot a chain embattled, for slavery, with a chevron *vert in* a chief engrailed, and three invected lines on a field *azure*, with the nombril points rampant on a dancette indented; crest, a runaway nigger, *sable*, with his bundle over his shoulder on a bar sinister; and a couple of gules for supporters, which is you and me; motto, *Maggiore fretta, minore atto*. Got it out of a book — means, the more haste, the less speed."

"Geewhillikins,", I says, "but what does the rest of it mean?"

"We ain't got no time to bother over that," he says, "we got to dig in like all git-out."

"Well, anyway," I says "what's some of it? What's a fess?"

"A fess — a fess is — you don't need to know what a fess is. I'll show him how to make it when he gets to it."

"Shucks, Tom," I says, "I think you might tell a person. What's a bar sinister?"

"Oh, I don't know. But he's got to have it. All the nobility does."

That was just his way. If it didn't suit him to explain a thing to you, he wouldn't do it. You might pump at him a week, it wouldn't make no difference.

He'd got all that coat-of-arms business fixed, so now he started in to finish up the rest of that part of the work, which was to plan out a mournful inscription — said Jim got to have one, like they all done. He made up a lot, and wrote them out on a paper, and read them off, so:

1. Here a captive heart busted.
2. Here a poor prisoner, forsook by the world and friends, fretted out his sorrowful life.
3. Here a lonely heart broke, and a worn spirit went to its rest, after thirty-seven years of solitary captivity.
4. Here, homeless and friendless, after thirty-seven years of bitter captivity, perished a noble stranger, natural son of Louis XIV.

148

Tom's voice trembled, whilst he was reading them, and he most broke down. When he got done, he couldn't no way make up his mind which one for Jim to scrabble onto the wall, they was all so good; but at last he allowed he would let him scrabble them all on. Jim said it would take him a year to scrabble such a lot of truck onto the logs with a nail, and he didn't know how to make letters, besides; but Tom said he would block them out for him, and then he wouldn't have nothing to do but just follow the lines. Then pretty soon he says: "Come to think, the logs ain't a going to do; they don't have log walls in a dungeon; we got to dig the inscriptions into a rock. We'll fetch a rock."

Jim said the rock was worse than the logs; he said it would take him such a pison long time to dig them into a rock, he wouldn't ever get out. But Tom said he would let me help him do it. Then he took a look to see how me and Jim was getting along with the pens. It was most pesky tedious hard work and slow, and didn't give my hands no show to get well of the sores, and we didn't seem to make no headway, hardly. So Tom says:

"I know how to fix it. We got to have a rock for the coat of arms and mournful inscriptions, and we can kill two birds with that same rock. There's a gaudy big grindstone down at the mill, and we'll smouch it, and carve the things on it, and file out the pens and the saw on it, too."

It warn't no slouch of an idea; and it warn't no slouch of a grindstone nuther; but we allowed we'd tackle it. It warn't quite midnight yet, so we cleared out for the mill, leaving Jim at work. We smouched the grindstone, and set out to roll her home, but it was a most nation tough job. Sometimes, do what we could, we couldn't keep her from falling over, and she come mighty near mashing us, every time. Tom said she was going to get one of us, sure, before we got through.

We got her half-way; and then we was plumbed played out, and most drownded with sweat. We see it warn't no use, we got to go and fetch Jim. So he raised up his bed and slid the chain off the bed-leg, and wrapt it round and round his neck, and we crawled out through our hole and down there, and Jim and me laid into that grindstone and walked her along like nothing: and Tom superintended. He could out-superintend any boy I ever see. He knowed how to do everything.

Our hole was pretty big, but it warn't big enough to get the grindstone through; but Jim he took the pick and soon made it big enough. Then Tom marked out them things on it with the nail, and set Jim to work on them, with the nail for a chisel and an iron bolt from the rubbage in the lean-to for a hammer, and told him to work till the rest of his candle quit on him, and then he could go to bed, and hide that grindstone under his straw tick and sleep on it. Then we helped him fix his chain back on the bed-leg, and was ready for bed ourselves. But Tom thought of something, and says:

"You got any spiders in here, Jim?"

"No, sah, thanks to goodness I hain't, Mars Tom."

"All right, we'll get you some."

"But bless you, honey, I doan' want none. I's afeard un um. I jis' 's soon have rattlesnakes aroun'."

Tom thought a minute or two, and says:

"It's a good idea. And I reckon it's been done. It must a been done; it stands to reason. Yes, it's a prime good idea. Where could you keep it?"

"Keep what, Mars Tom?"

"Why, a rattlesnake."

"De goodness gracious alive, Mars Tom! Why, if dey was a rattlesnake to come in heah, I'd take en bust right out thoo dat log wall, I would, wid my head."

"Why, Jim, you wouldn't be afraid of it, after a little. You could tame it."

150

"Tame it!"

"Yes — easy enough. Every animal is grateful for kindness and petting, and they wouldn't think of hurting a person that pets them. Any book will tell you that. You try — that's all I ask; just try for two or three days. Why, you can get him so, in a little while, that he'll love you; and sleep with you; and won't stay away from you a minute; and will let you wrap him round your neck and put his head in your mouth."

"Please, Mars Tom — doan' talk so! I can't stan' it! He'd let me shove his head in my mouf — fer a favour, hain't it? I lay he'd wait a pow'ful long time 'fo' I ast him. En mo'en dat, I doan' want him to sleep wid me."

"Jim, don't act so foolish. A prisoner's *got* to have some kind of a dumb pet, and if a rattlesnake hain't ever been tried, why, there's more glory to be gained in your being the first to ever try it than any other way you could ever think of to save your life."

"Why, Mars Tom, I doan' want no sich glory. Snake take'n bite Jim's chin off, den whah is de glory? No, sah, I doan' want no sich doin's."

"Blame it, can't you try? I only want you to try — you needn't keep it up if it don't work."

"But de trouble all done, ef de snake bite me while I's a tryin'him, Mars Tom. I's willin' to tackle mos' anything 'at ain't onreasonable, but ef you en Huck fetches a rattlesnake in heah for me to tame, I's gwyne to leave, dat's shore."

"Well, then, let it go, let it go, if you're so bullheaded about it. We can get you some garter-snakes and you can tie some buttons on their tails, and let on they're rattlesnakes, and I reckon that'll have to do."

"I k'n stan' dem, Mars Tom, but blame' 'f I couldn't get along without 'um, I tell you dat. I never knowed b'fo', 't was so much bother and trouble to be a prisoner."

"Well, it always is, when it's done right. You got any rats around here?"

"No, sah, I hain't seed none."

"Well, we'll get you some rats."

"Why, Mars Tom, I doan' want no rats. Dey's de dad-blamedest creturs to sturb a body, en rustle roun'over'im, en bite his feet, when he's tryin' to sleep, I ever see. No ,sah, gimme g'yarter-snakes 'f I's got to have 'm, but doan' gimme no rats, I ain't got no use f'r um, skasely."

"But Jim, you got to have 'em — they all do. So don't make no more fuss about it. Prisoners ain't ever without rats. There ain't no instance of it. And they train them, and pet them, and learn them tricks, and they get to be as sociable as flies. But you got to play music to them. You got anything to play music on?"

"I ain't got nuffn but a coase comb en a piece o' paper, en a juice-harp; but I reck'n dey wouldn' take no stock in a juice-harp."

"Yes, they would. They don't care what kind of music 'tis. A jews-harp's plenty good enough for a rat. All animals likes music — in a prison they dote on it. Specially, painful music; and you can't get no other kind out of a jews-harp. It always interests them; they come out to see what's the matter with you. Yes, you're all right; you're fixed very well. You want to set on your bed, nights, before you go to sleep, and early in the mornings, and play your jews-harp; play *The Last Link is Broken* that's the thing that'll scoop a rat, quicker'n anything else; and when you've played about two minutes, you'll see all the rats, and the sakes, and spiders, and things begin to feel worried about you, and come. And they'll just fairly swarm over you, and have a noble good time."

"Yes, dey will, I reck'n Mars Tom, but what kine er time is Jim havin'? Blest if I kin see de pint. But I'll do it ef I got to. I reck'n I better keep de animals satisfied, en not have no trouble in de house."

Tom waited to think over, and see if there wasn't nothing else; and pretty soon he says:

"Oh — there's one thing I forgot. Could you raise a flower here, do you reckon?"

"I doan' know but maybe I could, Mars Tom; but it's tolable dark in heah, en I ain' got no use f'r no flower nohow, en she'd be a pow'ful sight o' trouble."

"Well, you try it, anyway. Some other prisoners has done it."

"One er dem big cat-tail lookin' mullen-stalks would grow in heah, Mars Tom, I reck'n but she wouldn' be wuth half de trouble she'd coss."

"Don't you believe it. We'll fetch you a little one, and you plant it in the corner, over there, and raise it. And don't call it mullen, call it Pitchiola — that's its right name, when it's in a prison. And you want to water it with your tears."

"Why, I got plenty spring water, Mars Tom."

"You don't want spring water; You want to water it with your tears. It's the way they always do."

"Why, Mars Tom, I lay I kin raise one er dem mullen-stalks twyste wid spring water whiles another man's a start'n one wid tears."

"That ain't the idea. You got to do it with tears."

"She'll die on my han's, Mars Tom, she sholy will; kase I doan' skasely ever cry."

So Tom was stumped. But he studied it over, and then said Jim would have to worry along the best he could with an onion. He promised he would go to the nigger cabins and drop one, private, in Jim's coffee-pot, in the morning. Jim said he would "jis' 's soon have tobacker in his coffee;" and found so much fault with it, and with the work and bother of raising the mullen, and jews-harping the rats, and petting and flattering up the snakes and spiders and things, on top of all the other work he had to do on pens, and inscriptions, and journals, and things, which made it more trouble and worry and responsibility to be a prisoner than anything he ever undertook, that Tom most lost all patience with him; and said he was just loadened down with more gaudier chances than a prisoner ever had in the world to make a name for himself, and yet he didn't know enough to appreciate them, and they was just about wasted on him. So Jim he was sorry, and said he wouldn't behave so no more, and then me and Tom shover for bed.

CHAPTER TWENTY

Giving Warnings

In the morning we went up to the village and bought a wire rat trap and fetched it down, and unstopped the best rat-hole, and in about an hour we had fifteen of the bulliest kind of ones; and then we took it and put it in a safe place under Aunt Sally's bed. But while we was gone for spiders, little Thomas Franklin Benjamin Jefferson Elexander Phelps found it there, and opened the door of it to see if the rats would come out, and they did; and Aunt Sally she come in ,and when we got back she was a standing on top of the bed raising Cain, and the rats was doing what they could to keep off the dull times for her. So she took and dusted us both with the hickry, and we was as much as two hours catching another fifteen or sixteen, drat that meddlesome cub, and they warn't the likeliest nuther, because the first haul was the pick of the flock. I never see a likelier lot of rats than what the first haul was.

We got a splendid stock of sorted spiders, and bugs, and frogs, and caterpillars, and one thing or another; and we like to got a hornet's nest, but we didn't. The family was at home. We didn't give it right up, but stayed with them as long as we could; because we allowed we'd tire them out or they'd got to tire us out, and they done it. Then we got allycumpain and rubbed on the places, and was pretty near all right again, but couldn't set down convenient. And so we went for the snakes, and grabbed a couple of dozen garters and house-snakes, and put them in a bag, and put it in our room, and by that time it was supper time, and a rattling good honest day's work; and hungry? — oh, no, I reckon not! And there warn't a blessed snake up there, when we went back — we didn't half tie the sack, and they worked out, somehow, and left. But it didn't matter much, because they was still on the premises somewheres. So we judged we could get some of them again. No, there warn't no real scarcity of snakes about the house for a considerable spell. You'd see them dripping from the rafters and places, every now and then; and they generally landed in your plate, or down the back of your neck, and most of the time where you didn't want them. Well, they was handsome, and striped, and there warn't no harm in a million of them; but that never made no difference to Aunt Sally, she despised snakes, be the breed what they might, and she couldn't stand them no way you could fix it; and every time one of them flopped down on her, it didn't make no difference what she was doing, she would just lay that work down and light out. I never see such a woman. And you could hear her whoop to Jericho. You couldn't get her to take aholt of one of them with the tongs. And if she turned over and found one in bed, she would scramble out and lift a howl that you would think the house was afire. She disturbed the old man so, that he said he could most wish there hadn't ever been no snakes created. Why, after every last snake had been gone clear out of the house for as much as a week, Aunt Sally warn't over it yet; she warn't near over it; when she was setting thinking about something, you could touch her on the back of her neck with a feather and she would jump right out of her stockings. It was very curious. But Tom said all women was just so. He said they was made that way; for some reason or other.

We got a licking every time one of our snakes come in her way; and she allowed these lickings warn't nothing to what she would do if we ever loaded up the place again with them. I didn't mind the lickings, because they didn't amount to nothing; but I minded the trouble we had, to lay in another lot. But we got them laid in, and all the other things; and you never see a cabin as blithesome as Jim's was when they'd all swarm out for music and go for him. Jim didn't like the spiders, and the spiders didn't like Jim; and so they'd lay for him and make it mighty warm for him and he said that between rats, and the snakes, and the gridstone, there warn't no room in bed for him, skasely; and when there was, a boy couldn't sleep, it was so lively, and it was always lively, he said, because they never all slept at one time, but took turn about, so when the snakes was asleep the rats was on deck, and when the rats turned in the snakes come on watch, so he always had one gang under him, in his way, and t'other gang having a circus over him and if he got up to hunt a new place, the spiders would take a chance at him as he crossed over. He said if he ever got out, this time, he wouldn't ever be a prisoner again, not for a salary.

Well, by the end of three weeks, everything was in pretty good shape. The shirt was sent in early, in a pie, and every time a rat bit Jim he would get up and write a little in his journal whilst the ink was fresh; the pens was made, the inscriptions and so on was all carved on the grindstone; the bed-leg was sawed in two, and we had et up the sawdust, and it give us a most amazing stomach-ache. We reckoned we was all going to die, but didn't. It was the most undigestible sawdust I ever see; and Tom said the same. But as I was saying, we'd got all the work done, now, at last; and we was all pretty much fagged out, too, but mainly Jim. The old man had wrote a couple of times to the plantation below Orleans to come and get their runaway nigger, but hadn't got no answer, because there warn't no such plantation; so he allowed he would advertise Jim in the St. Louis and New Orleans papers; and when he mentioned the St. Louis ones, it give me the cold shivers, and I see we hadn't no time to lose. So Tom said, now for the nonnamous letters.

"What's them?" I says.

"Warnings to the people that something is up. Sometimes it's done one way, sometimes another. But there's always somebody spying around, that gives notice to the governor of the castle. When Louis XVI was going to light out of the Tooleries, a servant girl done it. It's a very good way, and so is the nonnamous letters. We'll use them both. And it's usual for the prisoner's mother to change clothes with him, and she stays in, and he slides out in her clothes. We'll do that too."

"But looky here, Tom, what do we want to warn anybody for, that's something's up? Let them find it out for themselves — it's their look-out."

"Yes, I know; but you can't depend on them. It's the way they've acted from the very start — left us to do *everything*. They're so confiding and mullet-headed they don't take notice of nothing at all. So if we don't give them notice, there won't be nobody nor nothing to interfere with us, and so after all our hard work and trouble this escape'll go off perfectly flat: won't amount to nothing — won't be nothing to it."

"Well, as for me, Tom, that's the way I'd like."

"Shucks," he says, and looked disgusted. So I says:

"But I ain't going to make no complaint. Anyway that suits you suits me. What you going to do about the servant-girl?"

"You'll be her. You slide in, in the middle of the night and hook that yaller girl's frock."

"Why, Tom, that'll make trouble next morning; because of course she' prob'bly hain't got any but that one."

"I know; but you don't want it but fifteen minutes, to carry the nonnamous letter and shove it under the front door."

"All right, then, I'll do it; but I could carry it just as handy in my own togs."

"You wouldn't look like a servant-girl, then, would you?"

"No but there won't be nobody to see what I look like, anyway."

"That ain't got nothing to do with it. The thing for us to do, is just to do our duty, and not worry about whether anybody sees us do it or not. Hain't you got no principle at all?"

"All right, I ain't saying nothing; I'm the servant-girl. Who's Jim's mother?"

"I'm his mother. I'll hook a gown from Aunt Sally."

"Well, then, you'll have to stay in the cabin when me and Jim leaves."

"Not much. I'll stuff Jim's clothes full of straw and lay it on his bed to represent his mother in disguise, and Jim'll take Aunt Sally's gown off of me and wear it, and we'll all evade together. When a prisoner of style escapes, it's called an evasion. It's always called so when a king escapes, f'rinstance. And the same with a king's son; it don't make no difference whether he's a natural one or an unnatural one."

158

So Tom he wrote the nonnamous letter, and I smouched the yaller wench's frock, that night, and put it on, and shoved it under the front door, the way Tom told me to. It said:

Beware. Trouble is brewing. Keep a sharp look-out.

UNKNOWN FRIEND

Next night we stuck a picture which Tom drawed in blood, of a skull and crossbones, on the front door; and next night another one of a coffin, on the back door. I never see a family in such a sweat. They couldn't a been worse scared if the place had a been full of ghosts laying for them behind everything and under the beds and shivering through the air. If a door banged, Aunt Sally she jumped, and said "Ouch!" if anything fell, she jumped and said "Ouch!" and before she'd get two-thirds around, she'd whirl back again and say it again; and she was afraid to go to bed but she dasn't set up. So the thing was working very well, Tom said he never see a thing work more satisfactory. He said it showed it was done right.

So he said, now for the grand bulge! So the very next morning at the streak of dawn we got another letter ready, and was wondering what we better do with it, because we heard them say at supper they was going to have a nigger on watch at both doors all night. Tom he went down the lightning-rod to spy around; and the nigger at the back door was asleep, and he stuck it in the back of his neck and come back. This letter said:

Don't betray me, I wish to be your friend. There is a desperate gang of cut-throats from over in the Ingean Territory going to steal your runaway nigger tonight, and they have been trying to scare you so as you will stay in the house and not bother them. I am one of the gang, but have got

159

religion and wish to quit it and lead a honest life again, and will betray the hellish design. They will sneak down from northwards, along the fence, at midnight exact, with a false key, and go in the nigger's cabin to get him. I am to be off a piece and blow a tin horn if I see any danger; but stead of that, I will Ba like a sheep soon as they get in and not blow at all; then whilst they are getting his chains loose, you slip there and lock them in, and can kill them at your leasure. Don't do anything but just the way I am telling you, if you do they will suspicion something and raise whoop-jamboreehoo. I do not wish any reward but to know I have done the right thing.

UNKNOWN FRIEND

We was feeling pretty good, after breakfast, and took my canoe and went over the river a fishing with a lunch, and had a good time, and took a look at the raft and found her all right, and got home late to supper, and found them in such a sweat and worry they didn't know which end they was standing on, and made us go right off to bed the minute we was done supper, and wouldn't tell us what the trouble was, and never let on a word about the new letter, but didn't need to, because we knowed as much about it as anybody did, and as soon as we was half upstairs and her back was turned, we slid for the cellar cupboard and loaded up a good lunch and took it up to our room and went to bed, and got up about half-past eleven, and Tom put on Aunt Sally's dress that he stole and was going to start with the lunch, and the next second she see me and she says:

"You been down cellar?"

"Yes'm."

"What have you been doing down there?"

"Noth'n."

"Well, then, what possessed you to go down there, this time of night?"

"I don't know'm."

"You don't *know?* Don't answer me that way, Tom, I want to know what you been doing there?"

"I hain't been doing a single thing, Aunt Sally, I hope to gracious if I have."

I reckoned she'd let me go, now, and as a general thing she would; but I s'pose there was so many strange things going on that she was just in a sweat about every little thing that warn't yard-stick straight; so she says, very decided:

"You just march into that setting-room and stay there till I come. You been up to something you no business to, and I lay I'll find out what it is before I'm done with you."

So she went away as I opened the door and walked into the setting room. My, but there was a crowd there! Fifteen farmers, and every one of them had a gun. I was most powerful sick, and slunk to a chair and set down. They was setting around, some of them talking a little, in a low voice, and all of them fidgety and uneasy, but trying to look like they warn't; but I knowed they was, because they was always taking off their hats, and putting them on, and scratching their heads, and changing their seats, and fumbling with their buttons. I warn't easy myself, but I didn't take my hat off, all the same.

I did wish Aunt Sally would come, and get done with me, and lick me, if she wanted to, and let me get away and tell Tom how we'd overdone this thing, and what a thundering hornet's nest we'd got ourselves into, so we could stop fooling around, straight off, and clear out with Jim before these rips got out of patience and come for us.

At last she come, and begun to ask me questions, but I couldn't answer them straight, I didn't know which end of me was up; because these men was in such a fidget now, that some was wanting to start right now and lay for them desperadoes, and saying it warn't but a few minutes to midnight; and others was trying to get them to hold on and wait for the sheep-signal; and here was Aunty pegging away at the questions, and me a shaking all over and ready to sink down in my tracks I was that scared; and the place getting hotter and hotter, and the butter beginning to melt and run down my neck and behind my ears; and pretty soon, when one of them says, "I'm for going and getting in the cabin *first*, and right now, and catching them when they come," I most dropped; and a streak of butter come a trickling down my forehead, and Aunt Sally she see it, and turns white as a sheet and says:

"For the land's sake, what is the matter with the child! He's got the brain fever as shore as you're born, and they're oozing out!"

And everybody runs to see, and she snatches off my hat, and out comes the bread, and what was left of the butter, and she grabbed me and hugged me, and says:

"Oh, what a turn you did give me! and how glad and grateful I am it ain't no worse; for luck's against us, and it never rains but it pours, and when I see that truck I thought we'd lost you, for I knowed by the colour and all, it was just like your brains would be if — Dear, dear, whydn't you tell me that was what you'd been down there for, I wouldn't a cared. Now cler out to bed, and don't lemme see no more of you till morning!"

I was upstairs in a second, and down the lightning-rod in another one, and shinning through the dark for the lean-to. I couldn't hardly get my words out, I was so anxious; But I told Tom as quick as I could, we must jump for it, now, and not a minute to lose — the house full of men, yonder, with guns!

162

His eyes just blazed; and he says:

"No! — is that so? Ain't it bully! Why, Huck, if it was to do over again, I bet I could fetch two hundred! If we could put it off till —"

"Hurry! *Hurry!*" I says. "Where's Jim?"

"Right at your elbow; if you reach out your arm you can touch him. He's dressed, and everything's ready. Now we'll slide out and give the sheep-signal."

But then we heard the tramp of men, coming to the door, and heard them begin to fumble with the padlock; and heard a man say:

"I told you we'd be too soon; they haven't come — the door is locked. Here, I'll lock some of you into the cabin and you lay for 'em in the dark and kill 'em when they come; and the rest scatter around a piece, and listen if you can hear 'em coming."

So in they come, but couldn't see us in the dark, and most trod on us whilst we was hustling to get under the bed. But we got under all right, and out through the hole, swift but soft — Jim first, me next and Tom last, which was according to Tom's orders. Now we was in the lean-to, and heard trampings close by outside. So we crept to the door, and Tom stopped us there and put his eye to the crack, but couldn't make out nothing, it was so dark; and whispered and said he would listen for the steps to get further, and when he nudged us Jim must glide out first and him last. So he set his ear to the crack and listened, and listened, and listened, and the steps a scraping around, out there, all the time; and at last he nudged us, and we slid out, and stooped down, not breathing, and not making the least noise, and slipped stealthy towards the fence, in Injun file, and got to it, all right, and me and Jim over it; but Tom's britches catched fast on a splinter on the top rail, and then he hear the steps coming, so he had to pull loose, which snapped the splinter and made a noise; and as he dropped in our tracks and started, somebody sings out:

"Who's that? Answer, or I'll shoot!"

But we didn't answer, we just unfurled our heels and shoved. Then there was a rush, and a bang, bang, bang! and the bullets fairly whizzed around us! We heard them sing out:

"Here they are. They've broke for the river; after 'em, boys! And turn loose the dogs!"

So here they come, full tilt. We could hear them, because they wore boots, and yelled, but we didnt wear no boots, and didn't yell. We was in the path to the mill; and when they got pretty close onto us, we dodged into the bush and let them go by, and then dropped in behind them. They'd had all the dogs shut up, so they wouldn't scare off the robbers; but by this time somebody had let them loose, and here they come, making pow-wow enough for a million; but they was our dogs, so we stopped in our tracks till they catched up; and when they see it warn't nobody but us, and no excitement to offer them, they only just said howdy, and tore right ahead to the shouting and clattering; and then we up steam again and whizzed along after them till we was nearly to the mill, and then struck up through the bush to where my canoe was tied, and hopped in and pulled for dear life towards the middle of the river, but didn't make no more noise than we was obleeged to. Then we struck out, easy and comfortable, for the island where my raft was; and we could hear them yelling and barking at each other all up and down the bank, till we was so far away the sounds got dim and died out. And when we stepped onto the raft, I says:

"Now, old Jim, you're a free man again, and I bet you won't ever be a slave no more."

"En a mighty good job it wuz too, Huck. It 'uz planned beautiful, en it 'uz done beautiful; en dey ain't nobody kin git up a plan dat's mo' mixed-up en splendid den what dat one wuz."

We was all as glad as we could be, but Tom was the gladdest of all, because he had a bullet in the calf of his leg.

When me and Jim heard that, we didn't feel so brash as what we did before. It was hurting him considerable, and bleeding; so we laid him in the wigwam and tore up one of the duke's shirts for to bandage him but he says:

"Gimme the rags, I can do it myself. Don't stop, now; don't fool around here, and the evasion booming along so handsome; man the sweeps, and set her loose! Boys, we done it elegant! — 'deed we did. I wish we'd a had the handling of Louis XVI, there wouldn't a been no 'Son of Saint Louis, ascend to heaven!' wrote down in his biography; no, sir, we'd a whooped him over the border — that's what we'd a done with him — and done it just as slick as nothing at all, too. Man the sweeps — man the sweeps!"

But me and Jim was consulting — and thinking. And after we'd thought a minute, I says:

"Say it, Jim."

So he says:

"Well, den, dis is de way it look to me, Huck. Ef it wuz him dat 'uz bein' sot free, en one er de boys wuz to git shot, would he say, 'Go on en save me, nemmine 'bout a doctor f'r to save dis one'? Is dat like Mars Tom Sawyer? Would he say dat? You bet he wouldn't! Well, den is Jim gwyne to say it? No, sah I doan' budge a step out'n dis place, 'dout a doctor; not if it's forty year!"

I knowed he was white inside, and I reckoned he'd say what he did say — so it was all right, now, and I told Tom I was a-going for a doctor. He raised considerable row about it, but me and Jim stuck to it and wouldn't budge; so he was for crawling out and setting the raft loose himself; but we wouldn't let him. Then he give us a piece of his mind — but it didn't do no good.

So when he sees me getting the canoe ready, he says:

"Well, then, if you're bound to go, I'll tell you the way to do, when you get to the village. Shut the door, and blindfold the doctor tight and fast, and make him swear to be silent as the grave, and put a purse full of gold in his hand and then take and lead him all around the back alleys and everywheres, in the dark, and then fetch him here in the canoe, in a roundabout way amongst the islands, and search him, and take his chalk away from him, and don't give it back to him till you get him back to the village, or else he will chalk this raft so he can find it again. It's the way they all do."

So I said I would, and left, and Jim was to hide in the woods when he see the doctor coming, till he was gone again.

CHAPTER TWENTY-ONE

Aunt Sally in Trouble

The doctor was on old man; a very nice, kind-looking old man, when I got him up. I told him me and my brother was over on Spanish Island hunting, yesterday afternoon, and camped on a piece of a raft we found, and about midnight he must a kicked his gun in his dreams, for it went off and shot him in the leg, and we wanted him to get over there and fix it and not say nothing about it, nor let anybody know, because we wanted to come home this evening, and surprise the folks.

"Who is your folks?" he says.

"The Phelpses, down yonder.'

"Oh," he says. And after a minute, he says, "How'd you say he got shot?"

"He had a dream," I says, "and it shot him."

"Singular dream," he says.

So he lit up his lantern, and got his saddle-bags, and we started. But when he see the canoe, he didn't like the look of her — said she was big enough for one, but didn't look pretty safe for two. I says:

"Oh, you needn't be afeard, sir, she carried the three of us, easy enough."

"What three?"

"Why me and Sid, and — and — and the guns; that's what I mean."

"Oh," he says.

But he put his foot on the gunnel, and rocked her; and shook his head, and said he reckoned he'd look around for a bigger one. But they was all locked and chained; so he took my canoe, and said for me to wait till he come back, so I could hunt around further, or maybe I better go down home and get them ready for the surprise, if I wanted to. But I said I didn't; so I told him just how to find the raft, and he started.

I struck an idea, pretty soon. I says to myself, spos'n he can't fix that leg just in three shakes of a sheep's tail, as the saying is? spos'n it takes him three or four days? What are we going to do? lay around there till he lets the cat out of the bag? No, sir, I know what I'll do. I'll wait, and when he comes back, if he says he's got to go any more. I'll get down there, too, if I swim; and we'll take and tie him and keep him, and shove out down the river; and when Tom's done with him, we'll give him what it's worth, or all we got, and then let him get ashore.

So then I crept into a lumber pile to get some sleep; and next time I waked up the sun was away up over my head! I shot out and went for the doctor's house, but they told me he'd gone away in the night, some time or other, and warn't back yet. Well, thinks I, that looks powerful bad for Tom, and I'll dig out for the island, right off. So away I shoved, and turned the corner, and nearly rammed my head into Uncle Silas's stomach! He says:

· "Why, Tom! Where you been, all this time, you rascal?"

"I hain't been nowheres," I says "only just hunting for the runaway nigger — me and Sid."

"Why, where ever did you go?" he says. "Your aunt's been mighty uneasy."

"She needn't," I says, "because we was all right. We followed the men and the dogs, but they out-run us, and we lost them; but we thought we heard them on the water, so we got a canoe and took out after them, and crossed over, but couldn't find nothing of them; so we cruised along up-shore till we got kind of tired and beat out; and tied up the canoe and went to sleep, and never waked up till about an hour ago, then we paddled over here to hear the news, and Sid's at the post office to see what he can hear, and I'm a branching out to get something to eat for us, and then we're going home."

So then we went to the post office to get "Sid;" but just as I suspicioned, he warn't there; so the old man he got a letter out of the office, and we waited a while longer, but Sid didn't come; so the old man said come along, and let Sid foot it home, or canoe it, when he got done fooling around — but we would ride. I couldn't get him to let me stay and wait for Sid; and he said there warn't no use in it, and I must come along, and let Aunt Sally see we was all right.

When we got home, Aunt Sally was that glad to see me she laughed and cried both, and hugged me, and give me one of them lickings of hern that don't amount to shucks, and said she'd serve Sid the same when he come.

And the place was plumb full of farmers and farmers' wives, to dinner; and such another clack a body never heard. Old Mrs. Hotchkiss was the worst; her tongue was agoing all the time. She says:

"Well, Sister Phelps, I've ransacked that-air cabin over an' I b'lieve the nigger was crazy. I says so to Sister Damrell — didn't I, Sister Damrell? — s'I, he's crazy, s'I — them's the very words I said. You all hearn me; he's crazy, s'I; everything shows it, s'I. Look at that-air grindstone, s'I; want to tell me't any cretur 'ts in his right mind's a-goin' to scrabble all them crazy things onto a grindstone, s'I? Here sich 'n' sich a person busted his heart; 'n' here so 'n' so pegged along for thirty-seven years, 'n all that — natcherl son o' Louis somebody, 'n' sich everlast'n rubbage. He's plumb crazy, s'I; it's what I says in the fust place, it's what I says in the middle, 'n' it's what I says last 'n' all the time — the nigger's crazy — crazy's Nebokoodneezer, s'I."

"An' look at that-air ladder made out'n rags, Sister Hotchkiss," says old Mrs. Damrell, "what in the name o'goodness could he ever want of —"

"The very words I was a-sayin' no longer ago th'n this minute to Sister Utterback, 'n' she'll tell you so herself. Sh-she, look at that air rag ladder, sh-she; 'n' s'I, yes, look at it, s'I — what could he a wanted of it, s'I? Sh-she, Sister Hotchkiss, sh-she —"

"But how in the nation'd they ever git that grindstone in there, anyway? 'n' who dug that air hole? 'n' who —"

"My very words, Brer Penrod! I was a-saying' — pass that-air sasser o' m'lasses, won't ye? — I was a-sayin' to Sister Dunlap, jist this minute, how did they git that grindstone in there, s'I. Without help, mind you — 'thout help! That's wher' tis. Don't tell me, S'I; there wuz help, s'I; 'n' ther' wuz a plenty help, too, s'I; ther's ben a dozen a-helpin' that nigger, 'n' I lay I'd skin every last nigger on this place, but I'd find out who done it, s'I; 'n' moreover, s'I —"

"A dozen, says you! — forty couldn't a done everything that's been done. Look at them case-knife saws and things, how tedious they've been made; look at hat bed-leg sawed off with 'em, a week's work for six men; look at that nigger made out'n straw on the bed; and look at —"

"You may well say it, Brer Hightower! It's jist as I was a-sayin' to Brer Phelps, his own self. S'e, what do you think of it, Sister Hotchkiss, s'e? Think o' what, Brer Phelps, s'I? Think o' that bed-leg sawed off that a way, s'e? I lay it never sawed itself off, s'I — somebody sawed it, s'I; that's my opinion, take it or leave it, it mayn't be no 'count, s'I, but sich as 'tis, it's my opinion, s'I, 'n' if anybody k'n start a better one, s'I, let him do it, s'I, that's all. I says to Sister Dunlap, s'I —"

"Why, dog my cats, they must a ben a house-full o' niggers in there every night for four weeks, to a done all that work, Sister Phelps. Look at that shirt — every last inch of it kivered over with secret African writ'n done with blood! Must a ben a raft uv'm, at it right along, all the time, amost. Why, I'd give two dollars to have it read to me; 'n' as for the niggers that wrote it, 'I low' I'd take 'n' lash 'm t'll —"

"People to help him, Brother Marples! Well, I reckon you'd think so, if you'd a been in this house vor a while back. Why, they've stole everything they could lay their hands on — and we a watching, all the time, mind you. They stole that shirt right off o' the line! And as for that sheet they made the rag ladder out of ther' ain't no telling how many times they didn't steal that; and flour, and candles, and candlesticks, and spoons, and the old warming-pan, and most a thousand things that I disremember now, and my new calico dress; and me and Silas, and my Sid and Tom on the constant watch day and night, as I was a telling you, and not a one of us could catch hide nor hair, nor sight nor sound of them; and here at the last minute, lo, and behold you, they slides right in under our nose, and fools us, and not only fools us but the Injun Territory robbers too, and actualy gets away with thats nigger, safe and sound, and that with sixteen men and twenty-two dogs right on their very heels, at that very time! I tell you, it just bangs anything I ever heard of. Why sperits couldn't a done better, and been no smarter. And I reckon they must a been sperits — because you know our dogs, and ther' ain't no better; well, them dogs never even got on the track of 'm, once! You explain that to me, if you can! — any of you!"

"Well, it does beat —"

"Laws alive, I never —"

"So help me, I wouldn't be —"

"House — thieves as well as —"

"Goodnessgracioussakes, I'd a ben afeared to live in sich a —"

"Fraid to live! — why, I was that scared I dasn't hardly go to bed, or get up, or lay down, or set down, Sister Ridgeway. Why, they'd steal the very — why, goodness sakes, you can guess what kind of a fluster I was in by the time midnight come, last night. I hope to gracious if I warn't afraid they'd steal some o' the family! I was just to that pass, I didn't have no reasoning faculties no more. It looks foolish enough, now, in the day-time; but I says to myself, there's my two poor boys asleep, 'way up stairs in that lonesome room, and I declare to goodness I was that uneasy't I crept up there and locked 'em in! I did. And anybody would. Because, you know, when you get scared, that way, and it keeps running on, and getting worse and worse, all the time,

and your wits get to addling, and you get to doing all sorts
o' wild things, and by-and-by you think to yourself, spos'n
I was a boy, and was away up there, and the door ain't
locked, and you —" She stopped, looking kind of wondering,
and then she turned her head around slow, and when her
eye lit on me — I got up and took a walk.

Says I, to myself, I can explain better how we come to
not be in that room this morning, if I go out to one side
and study over it a little. So I done it. But I dasn't go far, for
she'd a sent for me. And when it was late in the day, the
people all went, and then I come in and told her the noise
and shooting waked up me and "Sid" and the door was
locked, and we wanted to see the fun, so we went down the
lightning-rod, and both of us got hurt a little, and we didn't
never want to try that no more. And then I went on and
told her all what I told Uncle Silas before; and then she
said she'd forgive us, and maybe it was all right enough
anyway, and about what a body night expect of boys, for
all boys was a pretty harum-scarum lot, as far as she could
see; and so, as long as no harm hand't come of it, she judged
she better put in her time being grateful we was alive and
well and she had us still, stead of fretting over what was
past and done. So then she kissed me, and patted me on the
head, and dropping into a kind of brown study; and pretty
soon jumps up, and says:

"Why, lawsamercy, it's most night, and Sid not come
yet! What had become of that boy?"

I see my chance; so I skips up and says:

"I'll run right up to town and get him," I says.

"No, you won't," she says. "You'll stay right wher' you
are; one's enough to be lost at a time. If he ain't here to
supper, your Uncle'll go."

Well, he warn't there to supper; so right after supper
Uncle went.

172

He come back about ten, a little bit uneasy; hadn't run across Tom's track. Aunt Sally was a good deal uneasy; but Uncle Silas he said there warn't no occasion to be — boys will be boys, he said, and you'll see this one turn up in the morning, all sound and right. So she had to be satisfied. But she said she'd set up for him a while, anyway, and keep a light burning, so he could see it.

And then when I went up to bed she come up with me and fetched her candle, and tucked me in, and mothered me so good I felt mean, and like I couldn't look her in the face; and she set down on the bed and talked with me a long time, and said what a splendid boy Sid was, and didn't seem to want to ever stop talking about him; and kept asking me every now and then, if I reckoned he could a got lost, or hurt, or maybe drownded, and might be laying at this minute somewheres, suffering or dead, and she not by him to help him, and so the tears would drop down, silent, and I would tell her that Sid was all right, and would be home in the morning, sure; and she would squeeze my hand, or maybe kiss me, and tell me to say it again, and keep on saying it, because it done her good, and she was in so much trouble. And when she was going away, whe looked down in my eyes, so steady and gentle, and says:

"The door ain't going to be locked, Tom; and there's the window and the rod; but you'll be good, won't you? and you wont' go? For my sake."

Laws knows I wanted to go, bad enough, to see about Tom, and was all intending to go; but after that, I wouldn't a went, not for kingdoms.

But she was on my mind, and Tom was on my mind; so I slept very restless. And twice I went down the rod, away in the night, and slipped around front, and see her setting there by her candle in the window with her eyes towards the road and the tears in them; and I wished I could do something for her, but I couldn't, only to swear that I wouldn't never do nothing to grieve her any more. And the third time, I waked up at dawn, and slid down, and she was there yet, and the candle was most out, and her old grey head was resting on her hand, and she was asleep.

CHAPTER TWENTY-TWO

The old man was up town again, before breakfast, but couldn't get no track of Tom; and both of them set at the table, thinking, and not saying nothing, and looking mournful, and their coffee getting cold, and not eating anything. And by-and-by the old man says:

"Did I give you the letter?"

"What letter?"

"The one I got yesterday out of the post office."

"No, you didn't give me no letter."

"Well, I must a forgot it."

So he rummaged his pockets, and then went off somewheres where he had laid it down, and fetched it, and give it to her. She says:

"Why, it's from St. Petersburg — it's from Sis."

I allowed another walk would do me good; but I couldn't stir. But before she could break it open, she dropped it and run — for she see something. And so did. I It was Tom Sawyer on a mattress; and that old doctor; and Jim, in her calico dress, with his hands tied behind him; and a lot of people. I hid the letter behind the first thing that come handy, and rushed. She flung herself at Tom, crying and says:

"Oh, he's dead, he's dead, I know he's dead!"

And Tom he turned his head a little, and muttered something or other, which showed he warn't in his right mind; then she flung up her hands, and says:

"He's alive, thank God! And that's enough!" and she snatched a kiss of him, and flew for the house to get the bed ready, and scattering orders right and left at the niggers and everybody else, as fast as her tongue could go, every jump of the way.

I followed the men to see what they was going to do with Jim; and the old doctor and Uncle Silas followed after Tom into the house. The men was very huffy, and some of them wanted to hang Jim, for an example to all the other niggers around there, so they wouldn't be trying to run away, like Jim done, and making such a raft of trouble, and keeping a whole family scared most to death for days and nights. But the others said, don't do it, it wouldn't answer at all, he ain't our nigger, and his owner could turn up and make us pay for him, sure. So that cooled them down a little, because the people that's always the most anxious for to hang a nigger that ain't done just right, is always the very ones that ain't the most anxious to pay for him when they've got their satisfaction out of him.

They cussed Jim considerable, though, and give him a cuff or two, side the head, once in a while, but Jim never said nothing, and he never let on to know me, and they took him to the same cabin, and put his own clothes on him, and chained him again, and not to no bed-leg this time, but to a big staple drove into the bottom log, and chained his hands, too, and both legs, and said he warn't to have nothing but bread and water to eat, after this, till his owner come or he was sold at auction, because he didn't come in a certain length of time, and filled up our hole, and said a couple of farmers with guns must stand watch around about the cabin every night, and a bull-dog tied to the door in the day-time;

and about this time they was through with the job and was tapering off with a kind of generl good-bye cussing, and then the old doctor comes and takes a look, and says:

"Don't be no rougher on him that you're obliged to, because he ain't a bad nigger. When I got to where I found the boy, I see I couldn't cut the bullet out without some help, and he warn't in no condition for me to leave, to go and get help; and he got a little worse and a little worse, and after a long time he went out of his head, and wouldn't let me come anigh him, any more, and said if I chalked his raft he'd kill me, and no end of wild foolishness like that, and I see I couldn't do anything at all with him; so I says, I got to have help, somehow, and the minute I says it, out crawls this nigger from somewheres, and says he'll help, and he done it, too, and done it very well. Of course I judged he must be a runaway nigger, and there I was! and there I had to stick, right straight along all the rest of the day, and all night. It was a fix, I tell you! I had a couple of patients with the chills, and of course I'd of liked to run up to town and seen them, but I dasn't because the nigger might get away, and then I'd be to blame; and yet never a skiff come close enough for me to hail. So there I had to stick, plump till day-light this morning; and I never see a nigger that was a better nuss or faithfuller, and yet he was resking his freedom to do it, and was all tired out, too, and I see plain enough he'd been worked main hard, lately. I liked the nigger for that; I tell you gentlemen, a nigger like that is worth a thousand dollars — and kind treatment, too. I had every-thing I needed, and the boy was doing as well there as he would a done at home — better, maybe, because it was so quiet; but there I was, with both of'm on my hands; and there I had to stick, till about dawn this morning; then some men in a skiff come by, and as good luck would have it, the nigger was setting by the pallet with his head propped on his knees, and sound asleep; so I motioned them in, quiet, and they slipped up on him and grabbed him and tied him before he knowed what he was about, and we never had no trouble. And the boy being in a kind of a flighty sleep, too, we muffled the oars and hitched the raft on, and towed her over very nice and quiet, and the nigger never made the least row nor said a word, from the start. He ain't no bad nigger, gentlemen; that's what I think about him."

Somebody says:

"Well, it sounds very good, doctor, I'm obleeged to say."

Then the others softened up a little, too, and I was mighty thankful to that old doctor for doing Jim that good turn; and I was glad it was according to my judgement of him, too; because I thought he had a good heart in him and was a good man, the first time I see him. Then they all agreed that Jim had acted very well, and was deserving to have some notice took of it, and reward. So every one of them promised, right out and hearty, that they wouldn't cuss him no more.

Then they come out and locked him up. I hoped they was going to say he could have one or two of the chains took off, because they was rotten heavy, or could have meat and greens with his bread and water, but they didn't think of it, and I reckoned it warn't best for me to mix in, but I judged I'd get the doctor's yarn to Aunt Sally somehow or other, as soon as I'd got through the breakers that was laying just ahead of me. Explanation, I mean, of how I forgot to mention about Sid being shot, when I was telling how him and me put in that dratted night paddling around hunting the runaway nigger.

But I had plenty of time. Aunt Sally she stuck to the sick-room all day and all night; and every time I see Uncle Silas mooning around, I dodged him.

Next morning I head Tom was a good deal better, and they said Aunt Sally was gone to get a nap. So I slips to the sick-room, and if I found him awake I reckoned we could put up a yarn for the family that would wash. But he was sleeping, and sleeping very peaceful, too; and pale, not fire-faced the away he was when he come. So I set down and laid for him to wake.

In about half an hour, Aunt Sally comes gliding in, and there I was, up a stump again! She motioned me to be still, and set down by me, and begun to whisper, and said we could all be joyful now, because all the symptoms was first rate, and he'd been sleeping like that for ever so long, and looking better and peacefuller all the time, and ten to one he'd wake up in his right mind.

So we set there watching, and by-and-by he stirs a bit, and opened his eyes very natural, and takes a look, and says:

"Hello, why I'm at *home!* How's that? Where's the raft?"

"It's all right," I says.

"And Jim?"

"The same", I says, but couldn't say it pretty brash. But he never noticed, but says:

"Good! Splendid! Now we're all right and safe! Did you tell Aunty?"

I was going to say yes; but she chipped in and says:

"About what, Sid?"

"Why, about the way the whole thing was done."

"What whole thing?"

"Why, the whole thing. There ain't but one; how we set the runawaw nigger free — me and Tom."

"Good land! Set the run — What is the child talking about! Dear, dear, out of his head again!"

"No, I ain't out of my HEAD; I know all what I'm talking about. We did set him free — me and Tom. We laid out to do it, and we done it. And we done it elegant, too." He'd got a start, and she never checked him up, just set and stared and stared, and let him clip along, and I see it warn't no use for me to put in. "Why, Aunty, it cost us a power of work — weeks of it — hours and hours, every night, whilst you was all asleep. And we had to steal candles, and the sheet, and the shirt, and your dress, and spoons, and tin plates, and case-knives, and the warming-pan and the grindstone, and flour, and just no end of things, and you can't think what work it was to make the saws, and pens, and inscriptions, and one thing or another, and you can't think half the fun it was. And we had to make up the pictures of coffins and things, and nonnamous letters from the robbers, and get up and down the lightning-rod, and dig the hole into the cabin, and make the rope-laddler and send it in cooked up in a pie, and send in spoons and things to work with, in your apron pocket —"

"Mercy sakes !"

"— and load up the cabin with rats and snakes and so on, for company for Jim; then you kept Tom here so long with the butter in his hat that you come near spiling the whole business, because the men come before we was out of the cabin, and we had to rush, and they heard us and let drive at us, and I got my share, and we dodged out of the path and let them go by, and when the dogs come they warn't interested in us, but went for the most noise, and we got our canoe and made for the raft, and was all safe, and Jim was a free man, and we done it all by ourselves, and wasn't it bully, Aunty !"

"Well, I never heard the likes of it in all my born days ! So it was you, you little rapscallions that's been making all this trouble, and turned everybody's wit clean inside out and scared us all most to death. I've as good a notion as ever I had in my life, to take it out o'you this very minute. To think, here I've been, night after night, a — you just get well once, you young scamp, and I lay I'll tan the Old Harry out o' both o' ye !"

But Tom, he was so proud and joyful, he just *couldn't* hold in, and his tongue just went it — she a-chipping in, and spitting fire all along, and both of them going it at once, like a cat-convention; and she says:

"Well, you get all the enjoyment you can out of it now, for mind I tell you if I catch you meddling with him again —"

"Meddling with *who?*" Tom says, dropping his smile, and looking surprised.

"With who? Why, the runaway nigger, of course. Who'd you reckon?"

Tom looks at me very grave, and says:

"Tom, didn't you just tell me he was all right? Hasn't he got away?"

"*Him?*" says Aunt Sally; "the runaway nigger? 'Deed he hasn't. They've got him back, safe and sound, and he's in that cabin again, on bread and water, and loaded down with chains, till he's claimed or sold!"

Tom rose square up in bed, with his eye hot, and his nostrils opening and shutting like gills, and sings out to me:

"They hain't no right to shut him up! Shove! — and don't you lose a minute. Turn him loose! he ain't no slave; he's as free as any cretur that walks this earth!"

"What *does* the child mean?"

"I mean every word I *say*, Aunt Sally, and if somebody don't go I'll go. I've knowed him all his life, and so has Tom, there. Old Miss Watson died two months ago, and she was ashamed she ever was going to sell him down the river, and said so; and she set him free in her will."

"Then what on earth did you want to set him free for, seeing he was already free?"

"Well, that is a question, I must say; and just like a woman! Why I wanted the *adventure* of it; and I'd a waded neckdeep in blood to — goodness alive — *Aunt Polly!*"

If she warn't standing right there, just inside the door, looking as sweet and contented as an angel half full of pie, I wish I may never!

Aunt Sally jumped for her, and most hugged the head off of her, and cried over her, and I found a good enough place for me under the bed, for it was getting pretty sultry for us, seemed to me. And I peeped out, and in a little while Tom's Aunt Polly shook herself loose and stood there looking across at Tom over her spectacles — kind of grinding him into the earth, you know. And then she says:

"Yes, you better turn y'r head away — I would if I was you, Tom."

"Oh deary me!" says Aunt Sally; "is he changed so? Why, that ain't Tom, it's Sid: Tom's — Tom's — why, where is Tom? He was here a minute ago."

"You mean where's Huck Finn — that's what you mean! I reckon I hain't raised such a scamp as my Tom all these years, not to know him when I see him. That would be a pretty howdy-do. Come out from under that bed, Huck Finn."

So I done it. But not feeling brash.

Aunt Sally she was one of the mixed-upest looking persons I ever see; except one, and that was Uncle Silas, when he come in, and they told it all to him. It kind of made him drunk, as you may say, and he didn't know nothing at all the rest of the day, and preached a prayer-meeting sermon that night that give him a rattling reputation, because the oldest man in the world couldn't a understood it. So Tom's Aunt Polly she told all about who I was, and what; and I had to up and tell how I was in such a tight place that when Mrs. Phelps took me for Tom Sawyer — she chipped in and says, "Oh, go on and call me Aunt Sally, I'm used to it, now, and 'tain't ne need to change" — that when Aunt Sally took me for Tom Sawyer, I had to stand it — there warn't no other way, and I knowed he wouldn't mind, because it would be nuts for him, being a mystery, and he'd make an adventure out of it and be perfectly satisfied; and so it turned out, and he let on to be Sid, and made things as soft as he could for me.

And his Aunt Polly she said Tom was right about old Miss Watson setting Jim free in her will; and so, sure enough, Tom Sawyer had gone and took all that trouble and bother to set a free nigger free! And I couldn't ever understand, before, until that minute and that talk, how he could help a body set a nigger free, with his bringing up.

Well, Aunt Polly she said that when Aunt Sally wrote to her that Tom and Sid had come, all right and safe, she says to herself:

"Look at that, now! I might have expected it, letting him go off that way without anybody to watch him. So now I got to go and trapse all the way down the river, eleven hundred mile, and find out what that creetur's up to, this time; as long as I couldn't seem to get any answer out of you about it."

"Why, I never heard nothing from you," says Aunt Sally.

"Well, I wonder! Why, I wrote you twice, to ask you what you could mean by Sid being here."

"Well, I never got 'em, Sis."

Aunt Polly, she turns around slow and severe, and says.

"You, Tom!"

"Well — what?" he says, kind of pettish.

"Don't you what me, you impudent thing — hand out them letters."

"What letters?"

"*Them* letters. I be bound, if I have to take aholt of you I'll —"

"They're in the trunk. There, now. And they're just the same as they was when I got them out of the office. I hain't looked into them. I hain't touched them. But I knowed they'd make trouble, and I thought if you warn't in no hurry, I'd —"

"Well, you do need skinning, there ain't no mistake about it. And I wrote another one to tell you I was coming; and I 'pose he . . ."

"No, it came yesterday; I hain't read it yet, but it's all right. I've got that one."

I wanted to offer to bet two dollars she hadn't, but I reckoned maybe it was as safe to not to. So I never said nothing.

Out of Bondage

The first time I catched Tom, private, I asked him what was his idea, time of the evasion? — what it was he'd planned to do if the evasion worked all right and he managed to set a nigger free that was already free before? And he said, what he had planned in his head, from the start, if we got Jim out all safe, was for us to run him down the river, on the raft, and then tell him about his being free, and take him back up home on a steamboat, in style, and pay him for his lost time, and write word ahead and get out all the niggers around, and have them waltz him into town with a torchlight procession and a brass band, and then he would be a hero, and so would we. But I reckoned it was about as well the way it was.

We had Jim out of the chains in no time, and when Aunt Polly and Uncle Silas and Aunt Sally found out how good he helped the doctor nurse Tom, they made a heap of fuss over him, and fixed him up prime, and give him all he wanted to eat, and a good time, and nothing to do. And we had him up to the sickroom; and had a high talk; and Tom give Jim forty dollars for being prisoner for us so patient; and doing it up so good, and Jim was pleased most to death, and busted out, and says:

"Dah, now, Huck, what I tell you? — what I tell you up dah on Jackson Islan'? I tole you I got a hairy breas', en what's de sign un it; en I tole you I ben rich wunst, en gwineter to be rich agin; en it's come true; en heah she is! Dah, now! doan'talk to me — signs is signs, mine I tall you; en I knowed jis' 's well 'at I 'uz gwineter be rich agin as I's a stannin' heah dis minute!"

And then Tom he talked along, and talked along, and says, le's all three slide out of here, one of these nights, and get an outfit, and go for howling adventures amongst the Injuns, over in the Territory, for a couple of weeks or so; and I says, all right, that suits me, but I ain't got no money for to buy the outfit, and I reckon I couldn't get none from home, because it's likely pap's been back before now, and got it all away from Judge Thatcher and drunk it up.

"No, he hain't," Tom says; "it's all there, yet — six thousand dollars and more; and your pap hain't ever been back since. Hadn't when I come away, anyhow."

Jim says, kind of solemn:

"He ain't a comin' back no mo', Huck."

I says:

"Why, Jim?"

"Nemmine why, Huck — but he ain't comin' back no mo."

But I kept at him; so at last he says:

"Doan' you 'member de huse dat was float'n down de river, en dey wuz a man in dah, kivered up, en I went in en unkivered him and didn't let you come in? Well, den, you k'n git yo' money when you wants it; kase dat wuz him."

Tom's most well, now, and got his bullet around his neck on a watch-guard for a watch, and is always seeing what time it is, and so there ain't nothing more to write about, and I am rotten glad of it, because if I'd knowed what a trouble it was to make a book I wouldn't a tackled it and ain't a-going to no more. But I reckon I got to light out for the Territory ahead of the rest, because Aunt Sally she's going to adopt me and civilise me, and I can't stand it. I been there before.

THE END. YOURS TRULY, HUCK FINN.